MAGIC
IS FOR WHEN
YOU NEED IT

FLORENCE PETHERAM

AnnotationPress
A Division of WinePress Publishing

Annotation Press (a division of WinePress Publishing, PO Box 428, Enumclaw, WA 98022) functions only as book publisher. As such, the ultimate design, content, editorial accuracy, and views expressed or implied in this work are those of the author.

The author of this book has waived a portion of the publisher's recommended professional editing services. As such, any related errors found in this finished product are not the responsibility of the publisher.

ISBN 13: 978-1-59977-040-6
ISBN 10: 1-59977-040-7
Library of Congress Catalog Card Number: 2012930926

CONTENTS

ACKNOWLEDGMENTS

Many thanks to the following people who have made
helpful contributions to this book.

Norm Bunkowski, Certified Horse
Therapist who really knows horses,
Johnson Mininick, Program Manager of Yakama
Nation Cultural Resources,
Roy Novzari, Huna Instructor and skilled in
the use of the Pendulum,
Bette Lepp, friend with positive writing advice,
Esther M. Hamel, friend, Author of many books
who gave professional advice,
Shirley Aresvik, friend, Author and great "encourager,"
Peggy King Anderson, Teacher and Author,
Connie Epperly, Horse Trainer,
Noel Taylor, Horse Breeder,
Ronald M. Dodge, who gave helpful suggestions for chapters,
Henry Saffren, who grew up with horses and had
lots of stories to tell,

Kris Kovachev, who helped with final photo,
My children, Paula, Robin, Julie and Scott,
and
David Syverson, who used some "magic"
to make my computer work
and
David Thayer and the great staff at Wine Press Publishing
who made this book happen,
and
Titan, a very special horse.

CHAPTER ONE

BIG CHANGE

IT WAS TOO late now. She saw *that look* on her mother's face and Mandy knew exactly what it meant. No way was she going to change her mind. Here she was standing on the sidewalk in front of her house, packed and ready to go, and *that look* started to bring up feelings of guilt. It was clear her mother was unhappy about her leaving to spend the whole summer with her dad, but there was no going back. Her belongings were in her dad's Dodge pickup, where he was waiting with the motor running.

"I love you, Mandy Lee Hawkins," her mother said, hugging her. "I can't believe you're almost thirteen. You look so pretty and grown up in your new jeans and sweater. Oh, Mandy, I'm going to miss you. You call me if you have any problems at your dad's place and I'll come and get you, understand?"

"Don't worry, Mom, there won't be any problems," Mandy said, "I love you too." Mandy was proud of her mother and thought she was cool-looking with her curly brown hair and nice figure. She remembered when her mom and dad had been a good-looking couple together, but not anymore. Divorce had ended that.

Next she hugged her young brother, Alex. "Alex, from now on it's your job to take the garbage cans out on Wednesdays. Don't forget," she said. "Look after Mom and let Skippy sleep on your bed. I'll see you in July when you come for your visit with Dad. Okay?"

"Yeah, whatever," he said. "And, Mandy Pandy, don't you forget my birthday in June. I'm going to be ten." In a playful way he reached up and gave a little yank on her pony tail.

"Don't worry, I won't forget." She patted and kissed their Border collie Skippy on the nose. Then it happened. "Oh please no, please no, not now," she whispered. She watched her mother walk straight to the truck where her dad was waiting. Even though she couldn't hear exactly what they were saying, the tone was all too familiar. Why couldn't they just say nice things to each other instead of arguing all the time? She felt the beginning of a sick ache in her stomach like she used to get when her folks argued. It was as if there was a wall between her mom and dad. They jabbed at each other with words that bounced back at them, and nothing ever got solved. Fortunately, it didn't last long and her mother returned to the sidewalk.

After more quick hugs and kisses, Mandy and her dad drove away. She turned to look back at her mother standing under the maple tree in the front yard with her arm around Alex. They both looked sad waving to her. It wasn't fun leaving them looking like that. With one last wave she turned forward in her seat and let the feel of a new adventure come over her. She was on her way. Even though she was not quite thirteen, she felt newly grown up inside. A big change in her life had just begun.

The idea to spend the whole summer with her dad had been hers. Two weeks was never enough. She had secretly worried about him. Mom had her and Alex, but Dad didn't have anyone close to him. Maybe if she was there longer he'd miss the family and want to get back with Mom. She'd have the summer to work on that one.

For a while there was silence as her dad made turns onto Monroe Street. After a few blocks he pulled into the parking lot of a drugstore and stopped the truck.

"Why are we stopping?" Mandy said. "What's wrong?"

"Nothing's wrong, something's right," he said, smiling. From under his seat he pulled a package and handed it to her. "Here, this is for you."

The package was a small box wrapped in white paper, which Mandy quickly tore open. As soon as she saw the picture on the outside of the box she said, "Oh Dad," and leaned over to give him a kiss on the check. "This is way cool, a brand-new cell phone! Thank you," she said over and over as she hugged the package to her cheek. "You don't know how much I've wanted one of these. This is the kind my friends have, with all the new apps. Oh, Dad, this is so awesome!"

"I heard your mother tell you to call her. Now you can call or text her and Alex whenever you want. But remember, don't spend all your time on that thing. You'll have lots of things to do at the ranch."

Knowing she could call her mother on her new cell phone erased all guilt feelings about leaving home. She was ready for summer with her dad.

As they drove west from Spokane on I-90, the silence between them was interrupted when Dad blurted out, "Okay, Mandy, let's have it."

"What do you mean? Let's have what?" she said, turning to stare at him.

"Why all of a sudden did you decide you wanted to stay with me for the whole summer? I'd like to know because I don't understand. Don't get me wrong, I couldn't be happier to have you. I'm just curious about why you want to spend the whole summer with me instead of the usual two weeks. That's all."

Mandy sat speechless for a minute, looking straight ahead.

Dad looked over at her. "Is it because of some boy? Are you not getting along with your mother? Or is it something else? Which is it?"

Totally surprised by Dad's questions, Mandy took a quick look at him, her happy feelings starting to dim a little. *Oh no,* she thought to herself, *is this how it's going to be?*

"Mandy, I expect total honesty from you," he said. "When your mother and I divorced you were a little girl. You were nine. Now you're a young woman and things are different. I need to know why you decided to come for the whole summer. There has to be a reason. I'd like to know what it is."

Mandy, feeling and sounding defensive, looked right at her dad. "For sure it isn't because of any boy, and Mom and I almost always get along. So that's not it. I…I just had a feeling you might like to have me around for longer this time. I figured maybe you missed having Alex and me in your life and that you might like having one of us around for a little more that two weeks. So, I decided to come for the whole summer. That's all. And another thing, Dad, you need to know something I've never told you before. I really hate not having you in my life all the time. I get real lonesome for you and I miss you a lot."

With his eyes straight ahead on the road, her dad said absolutely nothing and gently placed his hand on her shoulder. Mandy watched a quiet look of pride spread over his face and the touch of a smile. He had the answer to his question. No other words or explanation were needed.

Dad let her listen to her favorite radio station and the time and miles went by quickly. They passed large fields of wheat and pastures with cattle and horses. He explained how important the wheat and apple crops were to the state of Washington. It reminded her of when she was little and he'd talk like this at their Sunday picnics. He'd tell them about plants and trees and rocks and make nature sound interesting. She loved that about her dad.

Finally, he merged south on US 395, and it wasn't long before they came in view of the Columbia River.

"Dad, I'm getting hungry. Can we stop at McDonald's?"

"We will," he said, "just as soon as you take a good look at that river over there that's thousands of years old."

To Mandy it looked like a big, blue-colored ribbon winding along. She'd seen it many times before. So, it was the Columbia River. "I'm looking, I'm looking," she said.

"That river you're looking at provides food, transportation, recreation, and power for a whole lot of us folks around here. It's because of that river that I'm able to have a small piece of land and grow things and live the way I want and have you come for the summer," he said.

She knew he was saying important things even though it sounded boring after a while, but she listened and pretended to be interested.

"Thousands of people drive by or over this river every day and never really see it," he said, pointing toward the river. "Look, there's the Cable Bridge. We'll be going over it in few minutes. Get in the habit of using your eyes, Mandy. Learn not only to just see, but use your brown eyes to really observe things around you. Some day what you see could turn out to be very important. Okay, that's enough from me. Dads are supposed to remind and teach their kids…right?" he said. He turned to smile at her.

"Wow, Dad," Mandy said, "traveling with you is like watching Discovery Channel."

"You think so? In that case, it's time for a commercial break."

They did stop at McDonald's and while Mandy was munching on a French fry, her dad turned to her and said, "Mandy, before we get home there's something I've got to tell you first. It's important."

By the serious tone of his voice, Mandy wondered again, *What now?*

"Only," he said with a big grin on his face, "that there's a great, big, important surprise waiting for you the minute we get home."

CHAPTER TWO
_____

TOTAL SURPRISE

"WHAT IS IT?" Mandy said, surprised by his announcement. "What's so big and important?"

"Wait and see," was all he said and started the truck.

"How about just one hint," Mandy begged.

"Okay, how's this? You're closer to your surprise now than you were five minutes ago."

"That's not fair," she said, laughing. "I want a really good hint."

"How about this? Your surprise is bigger than a postage stamp."

"Dad," Mandy said, "that's no help." The more she asked for clues, the more her dad responded with funny things that made them both laugh. "Okay, then don't tell me any more. Please, just hurry home!"

The trip from Spokane to Kennewick had taken about three hours. The last few miles for Mandy were now filled with eager anticipation. As they got closer she recognized familiar sights along the way. There was the yard with the miniature ponies, one with two beat-up trucks parked close to a double-wide, and another beautiful brick home with yellow flowers along the driveway. That's how it was in the country, she thought, a little bit of everything.

At last, Dad turned into the gravel driveway that led to an older two-story house set back from the road. Mandy liked where her dad lived. The place had a good feel. His property had a distant view of the Columbia River curving along in the background. There were pastures on both sides and an old apple orchard right across the road. It was a peaceful and beautiful part of the country.

"We're home!" Dad turned into the driveway.

"Good. When do I get my surprise?" Mandy said, practically jumping out of the truck.

"Hey, how about just as soon as you help get your things into the house," he said.

Mandy hurriedly carried her backpack and box of clothes upstairs to her room, dumped them on the bed, and raced back downstairs. After a few more trips from truck to the house, she called out, "I'm ready!"

"Come on then," Dad said. He led her out the kitchen door and onto the back porch.

Mandy secretly hoped her surprise would turn out to be a new bicycle, which was certainly bigger than a stamp. A new bike would be perfect. The roads around her dad's place were mostly good dirt roads that would be easy to ride on. From past visits she had met Maria Martinez, her same age, and her older brother Ricardo. They lived on a farm nearby. With a new bike she thought it would be fun to go riding with them.

"Now keep your eyes closed and watch the steps," Dad said. "There are three, so you'd better hang on to me. I don't want you falling down and breaking your nose or something before you get your surprise."

"Please hurry! I'm not going to break my nose and I can't wait any longer," Mandy said.

"Now we're going to walk a little ways down the driveway. Don't look until I say so. Just take it slow and easy and keep hanging on to my arm."

Mandy could sense with each careful step that her dad was having a good time with this surprise business. So was she. Several more yards down the dirt driveway her dad let go of her arm and commanded, "Mandy, stand right here. Don't move! Still keep your eyes closed and this time put your hands over your ears. When I count to three, open your eyes and put your hands down, or," he joked, "you can open your hands and put your eyes down. Got it?"

"Fun…nee, Dad!" Mandy said. Her eyes were tightly closed against the afternoon sun and her hands were pressed over her ears. Even with her ears covered she could hear some kind of scrambling and scuffling. *He must be getting the bicycle out of the barn,* she decided.

"I'm almost ready," Dad said. "Are your eyes still closed?"

"Yes, yes!" Mandy said impatiently. "Hurry up. I can't wait any longer!"

Then it began. "One…two…whoops, I have to start over," he said laughing, "okay…three! Now open your eyes!"

And she did! What she saw caused her to gasp, "No way!" Standing before her was not the bicycle she had expected, but a beautiful, brown horse with a white, crescent-shape mark on its forehead, staring straight at her.

On that warm June afternoon the world stood still for Mandy. She blinked her eyes and said in a choking voice, "Dad, you mean this is my surprise? Is it really for me?" In a million years she would never have guessed her surprise would turn out to be this beautiful horse.

"Yes, Mandy," Dad said. "It's really for you. This is your surprise. It's been waiting for you. First of all, it's a she. She's a five-year-old chestnut mare, and her name is Close. I know it's a funny kind of a name, but that's what she's called…Close. This is your birthday, Christmas, and glad-you're-here-for-the-summer present. When I saw her, for some reason I thought of you. So here she is and she really is all yours."

"Oh, Dad!" Mandy cried out, running to hug him. "This is awesome! She's the most beautiful horse in the whole world. Thank you! Thank you, Dad."

"You're welcome, Mandy Dear," he said, still holding the lead rope while accepting hugs from her. "I hear you and I'm glad you like her. I just thought that since you're going to be here all summer, having your own horse would give you something to do. That means learning to take care of her too."

Mandy, dazed from the gift of Close, stood perfectly still just looking at her horse. She barely heard what her dad said.

"There's a lot to learn about horses. You'll have to feed, groom, and exercise her. Shoveling out the stall will also be part of the program. You can begin by riding bareback. We'll get the right saddle for you later. For sure there's enough acres on the ranch here for Close to roam and eat, so don't worry about that. And remember your friend Maria Martinez? She has a horse too, so you'll have someone to go riding with. I think you're going to have a great time this summer with Close."

Before she took the lead rope her dad held out to her, Mandy stepped back to take a long look at the magnificent, large animal standing before her. She moved slowly toward Close. Looking directly at the horse that had not moved, she said in a soft voice, "Close, I'm Mandy, your new friend. I'm going to be looking after you from now on."

Close looked straight back at her with her large, dark eyes. Then in a friendly way, the horse lowered her head a little, gave a soft whinny, and took one step toward her.

In that moment Mandy knew for some reason she had been given a very special gift. With the horse nearer, her eyes were drawn to the white whorl on its forehead. The 'twisty' hair of the whorl was the perfect shape of a crescent moon. Fascinated, she moved closer and slowly raised her arm to touch the spot. The instant her fingers made contact with the horse, something astonishing occurred. For a heart-stopping moment, a zing-like energy streamed through her body, leaving her speechless and unable to move. It was like her heart opened up and became invisibly connected to the heart of this beautiful creature she was touching. It was like talking to Close without saying a word. It was the most incredible experience she had ever known. The only word she could think of to describe how she felt was…love. *What is happening here?* she wondered. She looked at her dad for an explanation. He smiled, totally unaware of her experience.

Mandy blinked as Close jerked her head away to one side. With a gentle snort she brought her large head back and laid it gently on Mandy's shoulder. Mandy did not move or speak, still feeling the powerful energy flowing between them. It was as if she and the horse were one. It was like they had known each other forever. She felt such a sense of love pass between herself and Close that it left her faint.

There they stood, horse and girl…a magical kind of connection between them.

"Well, if that isn't the darndest thing," Dad said. "I've never seen or heard of anything like that in my whole life. This horse acts like she already knows you. She came right to you like you were old friends. Horses don't usually do what your horse just did to you, Mandy. I don't understand it. Anyway, it looks like you've got a real friend. That's for sure."

Deep in her heart Mandy knew there was more to this horse than she could have ever imagined. For now, she sensed this surprise gift had come into her life for a reason. She didn't know why and wondered if it might have something to do with the almost magical experience she had just felt with this beautiful horse.

CHAPTER THREE

A FIND

OVER THE WINDING Columbia River, wheat fields, fences and orchards, over snowy clouds and wind farms, they flew through clean, fresh air. They looked down upon green growing things that sparkled and the whole world was brighter. Mandy felt herself smiling while she and Close galloped in her dreams all night long. The magical connection of Close filled her heart, and she was the happiest she had been in a long time. The unexpected gift of a horse had changed her life.

Early next morning Mandy hurriedly dressed in jeans and white tee shirt, fixed her pony tail, and ran out the kitchen door. She had to see if it was true, or had she just dreamed her dad had given her a horse named Close? Mostly she had to know more about the unusual connection between herself and her horse. Could it be that she dreamed that too?

It took her seconds to reach the pasture gate. To Mandy's great delight, standing in the morning sun looking at her with ears pointed forward was the beautiful Close. For a moment she just stood there and looked. It was true. This was the surprise gift her dad had given her. She didn't need to know much about horses to know this was one magnificent animal. Its beautiful, reddish-brown body all shiny in the sun looked as if it had just been groomed. Even the elegant sloping neck and muscular build was the mark of a special kind of horse. Without question she knew Close was not only beautiful, but one very smart horse.

She watched as Close flipped her mane and long tail in a movie-star sort of way and moved nearer. She knew it was the crescent spot she had touched yesterday that had given her that 'zing' feeling. But it was also the strong bond she felt for her horse that made her feel so connected. They had just met and Mandy already dearly loved and trusted Close and felt the feelings returned.

"Good morning, beautiful Close," Mandy said. "Last night I dreamed you and I went for a midnight ride and we rode all around here." She waved her arms in the air and smiled at her horse. Close stepped forward, gave a whinny, and gently placed her head on Mandy's shoulder just as she had done the day before. Mandy reached up to stroke the sides of Close's warm, soft neck. Oh, how she loved the largeness and feel of this beautiful horse! She was as comfortable with this animal as with any other human being she had ever been with.

Close kept her head on Mandy's shoulder for a minute then raised her head. She backed up and in a frisky mood pranced around Mandy as if inviting her to play. Flipping head and tail, Close trotted ahead in the dewy morning grasses with Mandy right alongside. Soon Mandy had to run to keep up. "Hey, Close," she called, "wait for me." What a wonderful everything Mandy thought, to smell the pasture, feel the fresh morning air blowing her hair, and to be running alongside her beautiful Close.

The wonderful everything Mandy experienced went on for several more days as she settled into her dad's home. She arranged her room with her things and helped with household chores as she learned more about her dad's routine. Being around Dad gave her a happy feeling. She loved all the attention he gave her and felt a little sorry that Alex wasn't there too. Every day she called or texted her brother and mom to tell them more about her horse. Every other free moment was spent outdoors with Close. *Dad is right,* Mandy thought. *There is a lot to learn about a horse.* She wanted to know it all.

Early one morning after brushing and feeding Close, Mandy took her out in the pasture and stepped back to watch what she'd do next. Usually Close wandered to a patch of grass and started eating. This morning she did something different. She headed toward a far corner in the fence that faced the road. Every few yards Close stopped, turned her head, and swished her tail to make sure Mandy was following.

"I can play this game, Close," Mandy said, running to keep up. "I'm right behind you." Nearer the fence along the road, Mandy saw something lying in the tall grasses. It looked like a big, old cardboard box someone had dumped over the fence. "Hey, Close! I said wait for me," yelled Mandy, speeding up. *That's weird,* she thought. No way would Dad leave a crumpled cardboard box in the pasture. She wondered why it was there and who could have tossed it there.

Before she could reach the fence, she watched Close bend her head down and nuzzle something in the box. Close quickly stepped back, tossed her head, and neighed nervously. "What is it, Close? What's wrong?" Mandy said. When she moved closer what she saw froze her to the spot. In the broken heap of cardboard, amid a swirl of buzzing flies and horrible smell, lay a black and white mother dog and three tiny puppies…all very still.

"Oh no!" Mandy cried out, feeling instantly sick to her stomach. She turned her head for a moment to keep from throwing up, but forced herself to look again. This was no time to be sick. At second look, it was obvious the curled-up puppies were dead. Bending down, she gently touched the mother dog with one finger and, to her relief, felt slight warmth. She touched the dog again in another spot to make sure. "Close, I think this one's alive. I've got to get help right away. Dad will know what to do. You stay here and watch over this dog. Okay? I'll be right back."

Mandy got up, and with heart racing, ran along the fence to the gate as fast as she could go. She burst into the kitchen where her dad was making coffee. "Come quick, Dad! Close just found a dog and some dead puppies by the front fence. They're all in a box. I think the mother dog is still alive."

"Well then, let's go," he said, putting the coffee pot down.

First he went to the barn and grabbed a wheelbarrow and old blankets, muttering to himself. "The blankety-blanks that dump their cats and dogs out in the country, thinking some nice farm family will take them in and pay for vet care should b...."

"Dad!"

"I mean it," Dad said and continued to grumble as they hurried to the pasture. "People like that should be arrested and put in jail and never allowed to have a pet again. If they can't be responsible enough for their animals they should at least take them to an animal shelter instead of leaving them out here to die."

In a few minutes they were at the fence where Close was standing near by. Still muttering, her dad carefully lifted the mother dog into the wheelbarrow onto a blanket. The dead pups he gently placed next to her. He shook his head as he covered them all. "Mandy, you're right. She's still alive. But honestly, I can see there's not much hope for this poor thing. It's too bad. You can tell by her color she was a beautiful-looking dog at one time. Look at her now. She's dehydrated and starved and almost dead. For sure her pups are gone. Nothing short of a miracle can save this one."

"Please, Dad," said Mandy. "She's still alive. Can't we try to give her some food and water? Maybe she's not as bad off as you think. Maybe a miracle will save her."

"I don't know about a miracle, but let's see what we can do."

Mandy walked behind her dad as he wheeled the dogs back to the barn with Close right behind. The only sound she heard in the bright morning was the bump-bump of the wheelbarrow over the pasture ground. The sound matched the bump-bump in her heart. She felt a sorrow for the mother dog in front of her who would never see or know her puppies. She felt like crying. It wasn't fair that those sweet little puppies would never be with their mother. What if she never saw *her* mother again? A deep sadness came to Mandy, and she wished with all her heart that her mother was here right now. It wasn't right. Kids and puppies should always be near their moms and dads.

Her feelings were interrupted by a sound behind her. The sound was a sad-like whinny. She turned to see her beautiful Close following right along.

"Look," said Dad, turning at the sound of Close, "even your horse knows this was a rotten thing to do to these dogs."

Chapter Four

A Promise

"MANDY, LISTEN TO me. This dog is not going to make it. Look at the poor thing," Dad said. "She's too far gone. I doubt she'll live 'til morning."

"There must be something we can do for her," Mandy said, close to tears.

"All we can do is take her back to the barn and make her as comfortable as possible. I'll fix a bed and you can try to get a little water down her. While you do that, I'll bury the pups. I warn you, Mandy, don't get your hopes up about this one."

The minute he said, "don't get your hopes up," Mandy did exactly that. Close had found this dog and there must be a reason why. Her mother was always saying there were no accidents in the universe. It could be they were meant to find this dog and save her. If the dog and puppies had been dumped in the apple orchard across the road, Close would never have found them. Instead, they landed on Dad's place, so there must be a reason.

Mandy helped her dad make a bed inside the barn where he tenderly placed the dog. With his fingers, he gently brushed off dried mud and dirt from the dog's body. Mandy's hopes shot up when the dog blinked her eyes a few times, proof she was still alive.

"See, she opened her eyes," Mandy said, patting her head. "The poor thing. I wonder what kind of dog she is?"

Dad looked up from his gentle cleaning. "For one thing, she's female. And I'd guess her to be a combination of breeds. Since she's mostly black with a little white around the head, she looks like a Border collie. With her long, slim legs and narrow head, she could have a little greyhound in her too. She's different looking for sure," he said. "It doesn't matter now. We'll never know."

It does matter, Mandy thought, and she was going to try everything possible to save this poor dog. She watched her dad and was glad for his help even though he had doubts.

From the faucet outside he brought a pan of clean water. "Try this," he said. "Don't force her to drink. The dog knows for herself what she can have. The poor creature is nothing but skin and bones. No wonder her pups didn't survive."

All morning Mandy sat on the barn floor and worked to give small amounts of water to the quiet dog. Carefully, she'd raised her head and held it in position so she could spoon a little water into her mouth. She'd wait awhile and then try again. With soft strokes of her hand, she brushed the dog's coat before covering her with a blanket. Leaning closer over the dog she said, "I'm sorry people left you out to die. I'm sorry your puppies are gone, but you don't ever have to worry again. You have a home now and I love you and you'll be safe here. Now listen, you have to get better. Dad doesn't think you can, but I do. Close found you and there's a reason you came to us." Mandy gently stroked the dog's head. "We'll both help you get well, and then you can sleep on my bed. Okay? Rest now and I'll be back in a little while. I promise." The minute she said the word, "promise," it clicked in…the name of the dog…Promise. "That's it," she said. "You sweet dog, you have a new name now. Your name is Promise."

The daylight hours Mandy spent between her horse and dog. Each time she entered the barn she hoped to see Promise up and about. So far, the dog lay sleeping, raising her head only for a little water. That's how the day went until her dad called her in for dinner.

Still thinking about Promise, Mandy glumly looked at the TV dinners her dad brought to the table. She didn't say anything and thought about the good meals her mom fixed at home and wished the whole family were back together. *Is this how it's always going to be?* she wondered. This was not the happiest of days.

As if reading her thoughts, Dad said, "Tomorrow night we'll go out for dinner. Then you can help me make a shopping list. We'll see what kind of a cook you are," he said. "You can see I'm not such a great cook."

That's the truth, Mandy thought. When the meal was finished, she excused herself from the table. "I'm going to say goodnight now to Close and check on Promise. Maybe she's awake."

"So the dog has a name now?" he said. "Mandy, I told you not to get your hopes up."

"Her name is Promise, Dad…Promise!" said a cross Mandy. "And I do have my hopes up."

"Promise? Where did you ever come up with a name like that anyway?"

"It's her name because I promised her we'd help her get well and keep her safe. Her name is Promise," Mandy said again in a loud voice as she walked out the door and headed straight for the barn.

Promise had not moved an inch. Mandy returned to her spot on the barn floor and began to caress the dog's head. "How do you like your new name, Promise? I've never heard of any other dog named Promise, and the name suits you just fine. You'd like my dog Skippy. I bet you two would have fun together." Mandy glanced toward the barn door and noticed it was getting darker. She hated leaving the dog but needed to say goodnight to Close. "I have to leave you for now and I'll be back in the morning. Good night, Promise," she said softly. "You get well now, do you hear?" With a final pat and kiss, Mandy left the black and white sleeping dog covered with a blanket and headed for the gate and Close.

In the pasture while she was hugging Close's warm neck, a surprise thought popped in her head. "Why not?" she said out loud. "Come on, Close. I've got an idea. You get to say goodnight to Promise too."

Mandy led Close through the gate and into the barn, hoping Dad would not hear the clomp-clomp of Close's hooves. There was still enough light coming through the barn door to see the still-sleeping dog. "Okay, Close, here she is," Mandy said, dropping the lead rope and bending to remove the dog's blanket. Close stepped nearer to Promise and jerked her head around with a soft snort and nostrils flared. She made no other sound and lowered her head toward the sleeping dog. Mandy moved back a little and wondered what Close would do next.

She watched as Close gently nudged the dog first with her lips. Then to Mandy's astonishment, Close began to lick the sleeping Promise with her long pink tongue. She licked her tenderly around the head and throat. Next, she licked up and down the back. Mandy watched spellbound as Close continued to lick Promise thoroughly around the stomach area and legs with long slow strokes. Still Promise did not move. Close licked and licked until the dog was shiny wet all over. When she was done she placed her forehead down to the dog's belly, stepped back, tossed her head and tail, and gave a soft nicker as if to say, "That's enough."

Mandy, wide-eyed, looked from dog to horse. She had never heard of anything like this…a horse licking a dog. What in the world had just happened here? Could it be the same love energy she had felt from Close? If so, what would it do for Promise? She covered the wet, sleeping dog and felt her heart fill with love for these two animals that had come into her life. She led Close back to the pasture and stayed a little longer in the darkness before kissing her goodnight on the nose.

On her way upstairs to bed Dad called to her. "Mandy, come down here please. I want to talk to you."

Mandy did not want to talk right now. She was in awe by what she had just witnessed between Close and Promise. Obediently, she came down the stairs and stood in front of her dad, arms folded. She was glad he was watching TV and had not heard her outside in the barn. She wondered what he would have done if he'd seen Close licking Promise.

"I'm sorry if I've sounded a little hard-headed today," he said. "You need to know this. Out here in the country things are different. Animals live and die all the time. That's part of life and we have to be realistic about it. I told you not to expect the dog to live. It's because I don't want you hurt when and if the dog dies. Believe me, Mandy, that's probably what's going to happen."

She could see Dad felt bad about hurting her. She leaned over and kissed him on the forehead. "Yeah, thanks, Dad. I hear what you're saying. I still think Promise has a very good chance to live and that's what I believe. Goodnight."

Mandy headed back up the stairs. It didn't feel right to tell him what had happened in the barn. There was no way to explain her belief of the healing spirit of her beautiful Close and how it had been used this night. She knew he wouldn't believe her anyway.

Halfway up the stairs her dad called back, "Mandy, don't worry. I'll check on the d…Promise again before I go to bed."

CHAPTER FIVE

ANOTHER SURPRISE

WITH HER FIRST thought of Promise, Mandy flew out of bed the next morning. She had to check on her dog. In her usual jeans and tee shirt she tip-toed quickly down the stairs. She decided to go out the front door around the side of the house so that Close couldn't see her. Care for her horse would come later.

She entered the barn hoping to see Promise awake on her bed. Instead, she was delighted to find the bed empty. That could mean only one thing…Promise was alive! She checked around the barn, expecting Promise to be near. She wasn't. Where was she? She had to be outside on the grass in the sun.

Mandy turned to leave the barn and that's when she saw it… the shovel. There it was, leaning against the door with bits of dirt and grass stuck to the bottom. Mandy felt a sick tightening in her stomach. "No," she cried out. "Please no!" But the dirty shovel before her told the whole story. Promise had died in the night and Dad had buried her so she wouldn't find her body. He had been right all along about her not living until morning.

Mandy slumped down next to Promise's bed. With her head down and arms around her knees, her feelings and thoughts came bursting out in a flood of tears. This was not how it was supposed to be. She had expected something miraculous to happen last night between her dog and horse, and it hadn't. She cried because she wanted Promise to live and now she was gone. She cried because she was lonesome for her mother and Alex and because her folks were divorced and Dad didn't live at home anymore. She thought she could make up for it by being with him all summer, but that wasn't working out the way she expected either. Homesick tears from her heart flowed down her cheeks, and she let them all come out.

After a while, her tears and sad feelings came to an end. *I can't sit here all day crying,* she told herself. She was deeply sorry for the loss of Promise, but the thought of Close changed her thoughts. After all, Dad had given her a beautiful horse to take care of. Instead, here she was inside the barn crying like a baby about something she couldn't help. Mandy didn't want Dad to find her like this either. She stood up, wiped her face with her hands, brushed the seat of her jeans, and left the barn without looking back at the empty bed and shovel.

The sight of her horse standing in the green pasture with blue sky all around and the bright sun immediately melted all sadness right out of Mandy's heart. It was a beautiful picture to see Close near the gate with head down as usual eating grass. Mandy watched Close in wonder as she moved slowly toward her horse. Close lowered her head up and down in quick moves and swished her tail and mane. Whoa, what was she doing? She wasn't eating. It looked like she was touching something lying in the grass in front of her. Mandy couldn't see what it was at first because of the grass. When she moved closer, she saw it. What she saw was black and white and moving. It was Promise! Mandy could hardly believe her eyes. It was Promise, and the dog's head was lifted up, touching Close's nose. Promise was alive!

Mandy practically flew over the fence. "Promise, Promise, you're okay," she yelled. "You made it! Oh I knew you could do it! You did it!" Back came the tears, all happy ones this time. She tried to hug Close and Promise both at the same time, which caused her to fall onto the grass laughing and crying for joy. With the morning sun in her eyes, Mandy lay in the grass, filled with happiness, staring up at Close and Promise. This was a miracle for sure. Promise had made it through the night and was alive. Now, both horse and dog were looking down at her as if they were saying, "What's with her?" This made her howl with laughter and cry out again, "Promise is alive!"

She got up and ran back to the house. Beneath her dad's bedroom window she yelled, "Dad, wake up! Come quick! You've got to see this!"

"What's going on, Mandy?" said her sleepy-sounding dad appearing at the window.

"Just come and see for yourself. You won't believe this. Hurry, Dad!"

"Give me a minute," he said. "I have to get dressed first." A few minutes later he walked out the back door rubbing his eyes in the sunlight. "Okay, what, Mandy?" Then he saw them. "Well, I'll be!" he said. He stared at Mandy and the skinny black and white Promise standing beside her. "That can't be the same dog that was lying in the barn all day yesterday. It's not possible."

"I told you she was going to get well," Mandy said, bending down to hug the dog. "I knew she would."

"This is unbelievable," said Dad, shaking his head with hands on his hips. "Totally unbelievable. I was wrong. It is a miracle, and you were right, Mandy."

Mandy and her dad spent the morning fussing over Promise. A new bed was made for the dog inside the kitchen. "We'll keep her inside for awhile," he said. He prepared a mixture of scrambled eggs, milk, and bread, which Mandy fed to Promise in small amounts. "She'll have to eat what's around here until we can get some good dog food for her," he said.

As she watched the dog eagerly gobble up the food, Mandy thought of last night, of Close licking Promise. For sure she knew in her heart it was because of Close's miracle touch that Promise was now alive and well. It was also one animal looking after another in a very caring way. Whatever it was, it was above awesome what had happened.

The rest of the day went by happily for Mandy. First, she'd run outside to be with Close, then back to the kitchen to be with Promise. Promise raised her head each time Mandy entered the kitchen. She licked her hand when she knelt down to pat her. Her animals were having a licking good time, she thought, and loved it.

"Okay, young lady," said Dad, "remember I said we were going out for dinner tonight? We'll celebrate Promise as a new member of our family. How's that?"

It was a contented Mandy who gently patted the now sleeping Promise as she and Dad walked out the kitchen door. It was okay to leave her now. Promise was alive and safe…just as she had promised.

CHAPTER SIX

SHOCKING NEWS

LOUD COUNTRY MUSIC greeted Mandy and her dad as they entered the Venture Inn, a restaurant popular with the ranchers and farmers in the Kennewick area.

"Hi, Bill!" Mandy heard her dad's name called from several directions as they made their way to an empty booth by a window.

"Wow, Dad, a lot of people sure know you in this place," Mandy said.

"It happens when you live in the country and we're all trying to make a living off the land. You get to really know your neighbors. Look around. You know some of these folks from your past visits," he said and waved to a couple in the corner. "There's John and Winnie Martinez. You know their kids Maria and Ricardo."

Mandy smiled and returned their wave. "Oh good. I want to find out if Maria, only I call her Ria, can come over and see Promise and Close. I haven't had a chance to call her yet."

Mandy was proud to be with her dad. He looked cool in his dark cowboy hat and jeans. His sun-browned face and beginning

29

gray hairs reminded her of an actor she'd seen on TV. Even his tiny bit of a belly didn't look bad.

He smiled when they were seated. "The folks in here who know me, and even some who don't, already know my pretty daughter is here for the whole summer," he said. "So see, how about that? Word gets out. You're famous."

"Really?" said Mandy with a big smile on her face.

"I told you that's the way it is around here. Everyone knows a little bit of everyone's business. I think they even know what I eat for breakfast," he said. "It's hard to keep a secret around here. The best part is if you ever need help for any reason, day or night, your neighbors and friends are right there for you no matter what. And that, Mandy Dear, is one of the reasons I like living here."

"That's so cool. You're lucky to have friends like that," Mandy said as she opened the menu. "What's good to eat here?"

"I'd say by the smells coming from the kitchen just about everything. Order whatever you want."

"I think I'll have macaroni and cheese," she said. "I want to see if theirs is as good as mine."

Her dad laughed out loud. "I don't think they make theirs out of a Kraft box like you do."

Their orders placed, they looked at each other and smiled. It felt comfortable being with her dad in a place like this with his friends all around. "Dad, I have to tell you that was so awesome how you helped Promise. Thank you."

"I didn't do anything special. All I did was fix her a bed and clean her up a little. You gave her food and water and looked after her. That was the important part. I still can't believe she survived. There's something unusual about how she recovered so quickly. We'll keep an eye on that one for the next few days and see what happens."

"What would you say if I told you that Close had something to do with Promise getting well?" Mandy asked in a serious tone. "I know it sounds weird, but it's a feeling I have about Close."

"I'd say that's interesting," he said. "On the other hand, it's not out of the ordinary for you to think that way. A vet friend of mine once told me that all young girls feel special about their horses. It's born into them he said, and the horses love the young girls right back. It's clear you and your horse already have a great connection. I'm proud of you, Mandy, but remember this…Close is not a horse out of some Disney movie. She's just a horse like any other horse. Don't start thinking she can fly through the air or some crazy thing like that."

Mandy didn't say another word. It was clear her dad would never understand about Close and Promise. Maybe it was just the way grownups thought. From now on, what she felt about Close she would keep to herself.

Their food arrived and they began eating. Mandy put her fork down and in an excited voice said, "Dad, do you think it would be okay if I asked Ria to go riding with me? She knows all the roads around here and she can show me what to do."

"Yeah, I think that would be okay," said Dad, taking a bite of steak. "We'll talk to the Martinez on the way out. And remember, always take your cell phone with you when riding. In case you fall off Close you can call for help"

"Don't worry, I'm not going to fall off Close," Mandy said.

"How's that macaroni and cheese anyway?"

Mandy smacked her lips in answer and watched her dad as he buttered a dinner roll. "You really like living here, don't you? And you're happy here too, aren't you?"

"Whoa, one question at a time," he said, looking at the roll in his hand. "To be honest, it's hard work. I've got payments on the ranch to worry about and the hay to plant and harvest. Then there's lease income to collect and a bunch of other stuff.

Without question, this is a great part of the state to live in. I've got the view of the Columbia River out front, an apple orchard across the road, and great neighbors all around. The best part is I'm working for myself. No one is telling me when to come and go. Yeah, I like it here," he said with a gentle kick under the table, "and I'm very happy having my daughter with me for the summer."

Mandy gave a half smile in return. She could tell he was happy living here on his ranch. Why couldn't he have felt like that when he was living at home with Mom?

While they were eating, more neighbors stopped by and exchanged friendly greetings. Mandy and Dad talked more about Close and Promise. They talked about her brother, Alex, and some of the fun times when her dad still lived at home.

"You know," Mandy said, "I think in one way Alex is glad I'm gone because Skippy sleeps on his bed now."

"Oh," he said, smiling, "I remember Skippy the day I brought him home for you two kids."

The conversation about home made Mandy lonesome for her brother and mother. She wished with all her heart that her whole family were here having dinner at the Venture Inn. With talk about family, another question came to mind. Now seemed like the right time to ask. "Dad, I've been wondering about this for a long time. Why did you and Mom get a divorce anyway?"

He looked away for a second, folded his arms on the table, then looked her in the eye. "Mandy, there are things that happen between a man and a woman that you're too young to understand. The easiest thing I can say is that your mother and I just grew apart. Your mother is a good woman and a good mother to you kids. That's all I'm going to say about it. Come on," he said, abruptly rising from the table. "It's time to go now. We'll stop and talk to John and Winnie Martinez on the way out."

As her dad fished money from his billfold for the tip, Mandy turned to see a man walking toward them. She hadn't noticed him before, but something about the man made her feel instantly uncomfortable. As he came closer, she saw he was about the same height and age as her dad. His faded denim shirt was rolled up to his elbows and he wore a pair of very old looking jeans and boots. His straw cowboy hat was worn almost level with dark eyes that revealed his unshaven face. But what caught her eye was the large buckle on his worn leather belt. It was shiny like silver engraved in a fancy design that spelled the words…Bad Company. Instinctively, Mandy felt this man *was* bad company and wondered why he wanted to talk to her dad.

"Hey there, Bill." His voice was loud as he clapped his hand on her dad's shoulder. "I hear it was you that got one of them there horses headed for the slaughter house in Canada. I hear it got loose or something. Too bad. That was part of my pay load headed for Canada and money right out of my pocket. But you sure got a good deal. How's it working out for you anyway?"

For one long minute there was silence in the Venture Inn… except for the country music in the background.

CHAPTER SEVEN

WHOLE TRUTH

COLD SILENCE ACCOMPANIED Mandy and her dad as they walked side by side back to the truck. He unlocked her door first and held it for her, then slowly went around to the other side and climbed in. For a long while they sat there in the darkness staring at the lights from the Venture Inn.

Dad was first to speak. He turned to Mandy and gently placed his hand on her shoulder. "I'm sorry you heard what that Dirk guy said in there tonight. He had no business shooting his mouth off like that in front of you and everyone. I don't trust that guy as far as I could throw him. Now let me tell you the gut-level truth about how I got your horse. It's time I told you."

With her hands folded on her lap Mandy nodded her head. She really did want to know. Maybe the tightness in her stomach would go away when she heard the truth.

"It happened right after you called to say you wanted to come for the summer. I got to thinking that since you'd be here that long you might like to have a horse to ride. So I decided to look around for one. I was going to ask some of my neighbors who have horses but didn't get a chance. The next day I happened to pass a field where some guys were loading up horses in a trailer. Most of the horses were weak and old looking and for the most part didn't look too good. I stopped anyway and found out they were loading them to take to the slaughter house in Canada."

At the mention of the words "slaughter house," Mandy hugged herself with her arms and uttered, "Ugh...gross."

"Wait, let me finish," he said. "Another reason I stopped was because there was one horse causing a problem, and I was curious to see what they were going to do about it. There was something different about this particular horse. It didn't look like the others. It was dirty and looked like it hadn't been fed for a while, but for some reason it had the smarts to not go up the ramp. Different guys kept trying. They pulled and pushed and whipped the horse, but no one could get it up the ramp. No matter what they did, it kept breaking away. It was all very interesting to watch. The guys kept screaming and yelling, trying to get the horse into the trailer with the others. It absolutely would not go in. Finally, at the last minute when they almost had it up the ramp, the horse got away again. That's when I got out of the truck to see what was going on."

Mandy kept looking directly ahead at the lights from the inn, still feeling her dad's eyes on her.

"I was told," he said, "there's a kind of superstition among the handlers that if an animal escapes on its own at the last minute, it's not meant to be slaughtered. If they force it, bad luck will come to the whole bunch of them. That's why they were all so determined to get that one horse into the trailer. You see, they get paid by the number of horses they deliver and they want as many animals as possible in one load. By the way, that's where that Dirk guy worked and why he knew about me. Anyway, I went over and talked to the guy in charge and asked if he'd be willing to sell the horse. He was only too happy to sell it because it took the superstition thing away. Besides, he didn't want to waste any more time on the horse. That's why

Dirk thinks I cheated him. Because now he wouldn't get paid for the horse he'd brought in."

Mandy's heart was pounding as she turned to Dad. "Well, that wasn't fair. You didn't cheat anybody. You bought Close honestly and saved her life. You didn't do anything wrong. How did you get Close home if she wouldn't get in a trailer for the other guys?"

"I called my friend Joe. He's an interesting guy. He's from the Yakama Indian Nation and lives and works around here. You'll get to meet him. He has a horse trailer and was able to pick up Close and bring her back here. Funny thing, Mandy, he told me that when he went to load Close into his trailer, all the guys were standing around taking bets on whether the horse would go in. Now that the superstition thing was away from them, they were laughing and having fun with it. Joe said they couldn't believe their eyes when Close marched straight up the ramp without one bit of trouble. Of course that made them mad because they thought they should have tried harder to get Close up their ramp."

Mandy smiled as she envisioned the scene of surprised looks on the faces of the guys who bet against Close going up the ramp.

"Before he left, Joe told me something else that was kind of odd. He said he felt that for some strange reason the horse sensed where it was being taken and wanted to come here to our place. Now isn't that crazy? I don't know what in the world that means or where the idea came from. That's what he said. Of course after Close arrived here, good food, grooming, and a pasture to roam in turned her into what you have now. That's the whole story of how your horse got a second chance. I'm sorry, Mandy Dear, I guess I should have told you sooner, but I didn't think you'd want to hear the gory part about the slaughter house."

For a long minute Mandy sat there. What her dad had just said was the answer to questions she had about Close. The information gave her a sense of relief knowing that Close really was a special horse. "Dad," said Mandy, feeling greatly relived, "thank you again for saving her. What you did was awesome. Close is ours and now she's safe at home and she's never ever going to a horrid slaughter house."

When they pulled into the driveway by the barn, the headlights showed Close once again standing by the coral gate waiting for them. A whinny and swish of her tail welcomed Mandy and her dad back home.

The thought that Close could have ended up in a slaughter house left Mandy feeling a little shaken. She needed to be with her horse right now. Her request to stay outside with Close was answered with a positive "yes" from her dad.

"I understand," he said, "I need to check a light in the barn anyway. Let me help you on Close first and don't worry. I'll look after Promise until you come inside."

Mandy climbed onto Close with her dad's help and laid flat down on the horse's warm back. With her arms around the mare's neck, she breathed in her earthy smell and felt her coarse mane rub against her cheek. "Oh, Close, Dad told me how he found you. I love you so much," she whispered. "I'm glad you didn't get in that old trailer. You were supposed to be here with me and Dad and Promise. You knew it too, didn't you?"

From Close came a soft whinny and Mandy felt the answer come to her. No words were needed. It was the same heart connection from her horse as before, and she knew without question her horse felt it too.

A crescent moon beginning to rise in the evening sky stayed with Mandy and the horse that had come into her life...until her dad called her in.

Chapter Eight

More Truth

A WHINE FROM Promise woke Mandy and she knew what it meant. The dog needed to go outside. She grabbed her phone, dressed on the way downstairs, and beat the dog out the kitchen door. It was a beautiful morning and a perfect time to be outside with her horse and dog.

She watched Promise move to the grass and was thrilled that the dog was alive. In just a few days she had responded miraculously to good dog food and loving care. Promise now slept at the end of her bed and followed her wherever she went.

Mandy let herself through the gate with Promise beside her to greet Close, who was prancing happily towards them. *What a great way to start the day!* she thought as she reached up to hug Close. Mandy moved her hands down the mare's chest, smoothing and gently massaging as she went along. She kept telling the horse over and over how beautiful she was. Close gave a little snort and nuzzled Mandy's neck, which tickled her and made her giggle. During all of Mandy's touching, Close had stood in the exact same spot. Mandy moved around in front patting her chest. Close brought her head up, and Mandy knelt down on the grass under her head stroking her legs. In total trust she wrapped her arms around the horse's front legs. "Oh Close," she said, "I love you so much. I just had to hug you this way." Close lowered her head and touched Mandy's head with her nose. That's when she got the idea to check out the belly of her horse. After all, Dad had said to use your eyes and observe things. She could see everything on top of her horse. Why not take a good look at the underneath of her horse as well?

Slowly she rolled over on her back, scooted down a little and was finally staring directly at the underbelly of Close. *How interesting,* she thought. Promise immediately lay down beside her after first giving a little "woof" greeting to Close.

With Promise next to her and Close directly above her, Mandy lay on the grass breathing in earthy morning smells of horse and dog. She had to admit this was way weird to be looking up at the underside of a horse. This was not where she expected to be when she woke up this morning, but here she was directly under Close's belly.

At first glance Mandy thought the whole underside reminded her of a big, brown, fuzzy blanket. She wondered about all that was going on inside that big body that kept moving with the rhythm of Close's breathing. She noticed the arc of the rib cage and the fine, long hair on the sides of the stomach. It made her realize there really was a lot to know about a horse. With one finger she reached up to brush away flies on Close's belly and marveled at the bigness and wholeness of this animal. It wasn't just her beautiful head or her warm comfortable back; it was the whole everything of Close she loved. This was awesome lying here with Promise in the shade under her horse. She felt totally safe knowing Close would never step on her or Promise. She decided to share this with someone.

From her jeans pocket she pulled out her cell phone and punched in her mom's number. "Hi, Mom," Mandy said, trying to sound mysterious. "Guess where I am right now."

"Hi, Honey," said her mother. "I don't have to guess where you are…do I? You'd better be at your dad's…right? And why do you sound funny?"

"I am at Dad's, and at this very minute I'm on my back on the grass looking up at my horse's belly," giggled Mandy. "I just had to call and tell you."

"Mandy," said her mother, "did you just say you're under your horse's belly?"

"Mostly all the way underneath," said Mandy. "Part of my feet are sticking out. Don't worry, Mom, I'm okay. I'm with Close and I was just curious to see what she looks like underneath. Mom, did you know a horse has a belly button too?"

"I'll take your word for it," her mother said, sounding relieved.

"Do you know what else a horse has underneath?" Mandy said.

"No, I don't," said Mom, laughing. "I don't need to know any more about the underneath personal parts of your horse. I think I can guess anyway. Listen to me. You get out from under there before you get hurt!"

Mandy, still giggling, promised her mother she'd be careful and would call back later. Before she could put her cell phone away she heard her dad yell from behind the gate. "Mandy Hawkins, what in the world do you think you're doing? Crawl away from under there. You and your dog are about to be stepped on by a 1100 pound animal! Whatever possessed you to get underneath that horse anyway?"

Mandy turned her head and said in a calm voice, "Dad, remember when you told me to always look at things around me? Well, that's exactly what I'm doing." There was no way her dad would understand how she felt perfectly safe on or under Close.

"Mandy, you've got a lot to learn about being around animals. Come on, it's time we took Promise to see Doc Barnes. His office called and said he could see us in an hour. For sure we know Promise needs to be checked out, and by the looks of things maybe you do too. So, get out from under there slowly now and let's go."

"Okay," she said, rolling out from under Close. *Dad has some things to learn about animals too,* Mandy thought. Wouldn't he be surprised if he knew what had happened between Close and Promise?

After a quick breakfast and change of clothes, Mandy fixed her ponytail and climbed into the truck with Promise on her lap. When they were on their way she said, "I've been thinking about Close. You told me how you rescued her, but I've been wondering what would have happened to her if you hadn't come along."

"Good question. I don't know for sure. Chances are good she would have ended up at the slaughter house in Canada anyway. And you know what goes on there."

"Gross!" Mandy said, her face screwed up in disgust. "I hate hearing about that place."

"The truth is that a slaughter house is exactly what it says it is…a slaughter house. I won't go into the ugly details, but it's where unwanted horses are taken," her dad said. "First of all, there's a great debate going on in our country about what to do with unwanted horses. You see," he continued, "there are people who think about horses differently than we do."

He went on to explain how people see the animals as either a source of performance or a source of food. He told her that there are some owners who take their horses to auctions because they don't want them anymore. If no one buys them, the horses end up at the slaughter house.

"I don't understand people like that," Mandy said. "How could anyone do such a terrible thing? I feel upset just thinking about it."

"There could be lots of reasons," he said. "One is because they flat out can't afford to feed their animal. Think about what happens to a horse when it gets old. It's not unusual for horses to live 20 years or longer. I know this one guy who had a horse named Sassy that lived to be 40 years old. It costs a lot of money to feed a horse these days. When times are tough families lose their farms and homes because they can't pay their mortgage. That means they can't afford to feed or house their animals either. If they have horses they may try to sell them or take them to an auction. They may even dump them at some rancher's place and hope and pray someone else will take care of them. It's like when somebody dumped Promise on our place."

"You mean people dump horses too?" Mandy asked in disbelief.

"They sure do," Dad said. "We're lucky, Mandy. We don't have to worry about feeding Close because we grow our own hay. Tell me now, where do you think all these unwanted horses should go?"

She thought before answering and said, "I don't know. There must be someplace for them, like an organization or someone who will take them."

"There are horse sanctuaries around, but not enough. Lots of folks think a slaughter house is better than letting a horse starve to death or die from some terrible abuse." Her dad sighed. "I don't know what the answer is either. Maybe just making sure if horses are taken to a slaughter house that they are treated as humanely as possible. Anyway, Mandy, Close doesn't have to worry about that anymore."

"She sure doesn't. You came along at the right time and saved her. Ugh, I don't ever want to think about her going to a slaughter house."

At the sound of the words, "slaughter house," the vision of the man with the belt buckle....Bad Company, flashed before her and Mandy felt a shiver of fear.

CHAPTER NINE

MYSTERY PATIENT

AT FIRST GLANCE Mandy was reminded of a slimmed down Santa Claus without the beard. He even acted like one as he bent down and introduced himself to Promise before lifting her in his arms. He was Doc Barnes, a veterinarian who had an animal clinic in Kennewick, and Mandy liked him the minute she saw him.

Mandy and Dad followed him into the examining room where he placed Promise on a table. While watching Doc Barnes with Promise, Mandy thought of the unusual licking the dog had received from Close. She had tried to tell Dad what she thought had been a healing caused by Close, but he had changed the subject. Maybe Doc Barnes would understand and explain it to her. She decided to wait and see if she should tell him.

They both watched silently as Doc Barnes examined Promise from head to tail. Not a sound did Promise make and stood perfectly still the whole time. When it looked like the exam was over, Mandy reached up and placed her hand on her dog's head and said, "Is she okay?"

"To tell the truth," he said, petting the dog's back, "she's more than okay. Her heart, ears, teeth, lungs, and eyes are practically perfect. Even her skin is in good condition...no ticks or lice. From what you've both told me," he added, "this looks like a different dog than the one you found in your pasture. Didn't you say this dog had newborn puppies when you found her?"

"Yes," said both Mandy and her dad.

"That's strange," he said. "Are you absolutely positive she had given birth to those puppies?"

"It sure looked like it," said Mandy's dad.

"Hmm," muttered Doc Barnes, slowly shaking his head. "That's most unusual. In all my years as a vet I've never seen anything like this. You both described finding this dog almost dead, then you say the next day she's up and running. It sounds like some sort of instant miracle-healing. Things like that just don't happen with the animals I work with. I honestly don't understand what could have occurred, but whatever it was, this dog is in fine condition."

There was her answer. The more she listened to Doc Barnes, the more she decided to keep quiet about what had happened between her horse and dog. She was absolutely positive he would not believe her if she told what had taken place in the barn. Once again she'd keep the secret of Close in her heart.

"That's all I can say. Oh well, we'll never know. Incidentally," he said, looking at Mandy's dad, "you guessed right. Your dog is a mix of Border collie and greyhound. It's an interesting mix. It means she's one smart dog and can run like the wind."

"By the way, Mandy," he said, "I hear you have a new mare at your place. How do you like her?"

"My horse is awesome and Dad saved her from the slaughter house," Mandy said, smiling proudly at her dad. "I've started to ride bareback and she's beautiful. Her name is Close and she's very special."

"Tell me young lady," Doc Barnes said, "do you wear a helmet when you ride your horse bareback?"

"No," Mandy said, "I thought helmets were just for motorcycle and bike riders."

"Not so. As a vet I've seen too many accidents with horses and riders. Most of the time the horse is okay, but the rider ends up in the hospital with some kind of head injury. Take my advice. Don't ever ride your horse without wearing a helmet. I'm very serious about this, Mandy."

"I'll see to that," Mandy's dad said, placing his hand on her head and giving it a little shake. "We'll get one today."

"Good," he said, "and don't forget, if your horse or dog ever needs attention, give me a call. Speaking of horses, did you know your neighbor Henry Dolan has acquired some new Thoroughbreds at his place? Have you seen them yet? He's got some real dandies. You should go take a look at them when you get a chance."

"Thanks, we will," said Dad.

Doc Barnes snapped a leash onto Promise's new collar and lifted the dog to the floor. "Forget the bill," he said, handing the leash to Mandy. "There's no charge for this once-in-a-lifetime mystery patient. There wasn't anything wrong with her really. She's a real sweetheart, just needs some fattening up is all."

Mandy guided Promise out of the examining room followed by her dad, who was thanking Doc Barnes, who was still shaking his head. When they were out the door Mandy said, "I don't think Doc Barnes believed us about the puppies."

"We told him the truth," said Dad, "that's all we could do."

Not all the truth, Mandy thought to herself. *When they found Promise, she was dying. After Close licked her all over, she survived.* Mandy believed the real truth was the healing energy that had come from her horse. She had been there and seen it with her own eyes. She was quiet on the way home in spite of Promise trying to lick her face. It was her dad who did all the talking.

"Good, now we know about Promise. It looks like I made a big mistake in judgment. Look at her. She sure doesn't look like the same dog, does she? I guess it's one for the books," he said.

When the truck pulled into the driveway, Mandy saw Close standing by the gate, swishing her tail and looking at them. "Look! There she is waiting for us. That's so cool how she knows we're home."

"Seems to me," Dad said as he lifted Promise out of the truck, "that horse of yours does that all the time."

Promise shook her skinny body and with surprising speed ran to the gate straight for Close. To their amazement she squeezed under the gate, shook herself again, and trotted over to stand directly in front of Close. She looked up at the horse whose head bent down to hers, and their noses touched for what seemed like a very long time.

Mandy said nothing as she walked toward the gate. She was glad Dad hadn't followed. Leaning against the gate she stood there watching Promise and Close together. It was a beautiful sight. Without question Promise knew Close had saved her life. This was her way was saying "thank you."

Was this the truth or what? Did Close really have some kind of healing gift? Was Mandy just imagining all of this? What was she supposed to do? While wondering about all of this, Mandy's cell phone rang. To her surprise it was Ria. Since she'd been at her dad's she'd tried to call her several times, but there had been no answer. "Oh hi, Ria. I was wondering where you were. I have a whole lot of cool stuff to tell you. By any chance can you come over tonight?" Mandy asked.

"Yeah, that will be okay. I'll ask Dad to bring me over after supper. And I have a lot of stuff to tell you too," Ria said in a sad voice.

What was that all about? Mandy wondered. Ria didn't sound too good. Something pretty awful must have happened to cause her to sound so sad. Oh well, she'd find out tonight.

CHAPTER TEN

SAD NEWS

DINNER WAS ANOTHER of the frozen kind prepared by Dad in the microwave. This time there was a difference… there was salad…her salad. She had carefully cut up lettuce, cucumbers, and tomatoes, added dressing and put in salad bowls for each of them. Mandy looked at the food in the black plastic containers and wondered again what her mom and Alex were having for dinner. For sure it wouldn't be anything like this. She had just texted Alex and he'd texted back about 'good smells' coming from the kitchen.

"Hey, good job on the salad," Dad said, taking a big bite after they were seated at the table.

"Thanks, it's the same kind Mom makes." To herself she said, "remember?" Being with her dad for the summer was bringing up all kinds of mixed feelings about her family. Right now Mandy had resentful feelings. If Mom and Dad hadn't divorced, they'd all be having a 'good smells' dinner and it wouldn't be in black plastic dishes. She sighed and looked down at the lasagna. Her hunger took over and she began to eat.

"Mandy, remember when I told you about Joe?"

She nodded her head.

"He's coming by tomorrow. I want you to know in case I'm not here. He'll be looking over the property."

"Why?"

"Because I might need to drill for another well on the place and Joe can figure out where it should be." Taking another bite of his salad, he added, "If you're lucky and if he has time, he might tell you some stories about the Yakama Indian Nation. He grew up on the reservation where he and his dad were horse traders, so he knows a lot about horses. His Indian name is Joe-Many-Horses."

"Yeah okay, I'll probably be outside with Close and Promise anyway."

While Mandy was cleaning up after dinner, she could see Close and Promise in the pasture from the kitchen window. It was fun to watch the two together. Close lowered her head down to Promise's nose as if they were kissing. After watching them several times, she decided that's what they were doing. *There isn't any reason why animals couldn't kiss or smile,* she thought. *If they have lips they could do it.*

Mandy especially liked the times when Close would kneel, then roll over on her back. She'd grind her back on the ground, kick her legs in the air, then roll back up. Grass and dirt would go flying in a cloud as she shook her mane and tail. Then she'd get up and do it all over again. The part that was really funny was when Promise would roll on her back and do the very same thing beside her. It was easy to see they were friends having fun with each other. It made Mandy smile.

She finished in the kitchen in time to see the Martinez pickup truck pull into the driveway. Before she could get out the door, Dad was outside greeting Mr. Martinez.

"Hi, Ria," Mandy called as she walked out to meet her. The last time she had seen Ria and her brother Rick was during Christmas vacation. Ria looked even prettier now in her bright yellow tee shirt and jeans. Her straight, shiny black hair was shoulder length and she looked like a TV shampoo commercial. Ria was about the same height as herself and also had brown eyes.

"Ria, great to see you. Hey, your hair is a lot longer since the last time I saw you."

Ria grinned and hugged Mandy. "Yeah, and so is yours. And where did you get that cool-looking shirt?"

"Oh, this? Mom got it for me. She said I had to dress nice around dad's friends. Do I look nice enough around you? Now tell me the honest truth."

They both laughed and continued with more 'cools and ahs' of admiration of each other's hair and clothes.

"Now come this way, Ria. You've got to see my horse Close and dog Promise. They're over here in the pasture," said Mandy, leading the way.

"Good, I want to see Close up close," Ria said.

They walked toward the pasture and Mandy pointed to Close, who gave the girls a friendly neigh and shake of her head while Promise's greeting was a wagging tail.

"Oh, Mandy, she's way cool," Ria said and reached out with fingertips to touch Close's neck. Ria made some comparisons of her horse Fern to Close and more horse talk followed between the girls. They talked about having to wear helmets while riding and how long it took to groom their horses and how they least liked the clean-up part. So far it was all happy horse talk.

Mandy moved over and while gently combing Close's mane with her fingers said, "How's Rick? Mandy secretly liked Ria's brother and thought he was really good looking.

Ria's face clouded over at the mention of her brother. It brought back the sadness in her voice. "Right now we're all worried about Rick," she said. "Maybe you've heard, Rick has cancer."

"No," said Mandy, totally caught off guard by the news. "But he can't. He's too young." Her heart gave an extra thud as she thought of someone as young as Rick getting cancer. "I thought only old people and women got cancer," she added.

"Not true. I've learned that anyone can get it at any age," said Ria, "and right now it doesn't look too good for Rick."

For a few moments there was silence between them. Mandy now knew the reason for Ria's sadness. She felt sorry for her friend and brother. The sorry feeling came from a space in her heart she couldn't express. What would she do if that happened to her brother Alex? Just thinking about it made her stomach tighten up.

"Is Rick in bed? Is he hurting real bad?

"No, not exactly," Ria said, with fingers still on Close's neck. "He's tired all the time and can't do stuff like he used to do. Like he used to tease me a lot and make me laugh. He doesn't do that anymore. That's how I can tell he's not feeling good."

"What do the doctors say? Maybe they're wrong."

"He had tests done in Seattle, and now they say he has to come back for more tests. The worst part is that Rick was planning to turn out for the Kennewick High School baseball team and now he can't. We're not sure if he'll even be able to start school this fall."

Both girls still had their hands on Close, who had not moved except for the twitching of her forward bent ears. Feeling bad for her friend and not sure what to say, Mandy changed the subject. "Ria, do you think it would be fun if we went riding together? You can teach me what to do. It'll have to be bareback though. I haven't been fitted for a saddle yet. Dad said that will come later. Would that be okay with you?"

"Cool," Ria said, pointing her finger at Mandy and saying in a funky voice, "now the first thing you have to do is wear a helmet and the next you have to do is…" Both girls burst out laughing.

Releasing her fingers from Close's mane, Ria said with her eyes still on Close, "Funny thing, I have a feeling that your horse has been listening to our every word. Look, see how her ears are turned forward and how she's looking at us. Do you think horses understand what people think and say? Horses don't do that, do they?"

Mandy shrugged her shoulders as she gently reached to touch the tip of Close's ears. "Maybe," she said. "I think some dogs and horses are pretty smart that way." Without question, she knew for sure that her Close had been listening to every single word.

CHAPTER ELEVEN

INVITATION

"RICK-HAS-CANCER," were the sad words heard over and over in Mandy's head. They became a rhythm for grooming Close. Her arms stretched up and down as her body moved in motion to the words and brush. All the while she was thinking about Rick, she barely heard the satisfying snorts and grunts coming from Close or the sound of a meadowlark announcing the morning.

"Mandy!" The sound of her name so startled her she dropped the brush, which caused Close to jump forward.

"Dad, you scared me!"

"Sorry, I didn't mean to scare you," he said, walking up behind her. "By the way, I can tell Close really likes how you groom her by how she stands."

"Thanks," Mandy said, picking up the brush. "I just brush the hair down the way the hair grows like you showed me. I always brush her after a ride, but she likes it in the morning too. Dad, I've been thinking about Rick and I was..."

"Look, Mandy, we talked about this last night. The Martinez family is doing all the right things to take care of Rick. They have the best doctors who know what they're doing. There's nothing we can do, so stop worrying. I mean it. It's all in the hands of doctors and the good Lord above. I have a feeling Rick will be okay. We just have to think positive about him. Now the reason I came out here was to tell you some news I think you'll like," he said. "No frozen meals for tomorrow night. We're going out for dinner."

"Cool. Where are we going?" she asked, remembering the last dinner and a certain man wearing a certain belt buckle.

"To a nice restaurant in town. I've made reservations for the three of us," said Dad.

"The three of us? Who else is coming?"

"I've invited a special lady friend of mine to join us. I'm anxious to have you meet her. Her name is Ellie, and I know you're going to like her."

Mandy noticed Dad's voice changed slightly and his face brightened as he talked about Ellie. He sounded happier in a way which caused her to feel resentful toward the lady already. So this was why he was happy living here…a special lady friend. *Why couldn't he have looked and sounded that way around Mom?* she wondered.

"Okay, I'll meet her, but I don't really need to go," Mandy said, continuing to brush Close. To herself she thought…*and I don't have to like the lady either.* "You two go ahead. I'm okay here with Close and Promise." There was no way she wanted to spend time with someone who might be taking the place of her mother. She'd much rather be right here at home with her horse and dog.

Her dad moved his head closer to Mandy and said calmly but firmly, "Maybe you didn't hear me. I said her name is Ellie and she'll be joining *us* for dinner. That means there will be three of us…you…me and Ellie. There will be no ifs, ands, or buts about it. Give this lady a chance, Mandy. That's all I ask. You'll like her, I promise. Wait and see."

With those words, he turned his back and headed for the house. "Oh, and a reminder," he said, turning around, "Joe will be stopping by sometime tomorrow morning to look over the property."

Mandy kept right on brushing. Without turning to look at her dad, she returned a not-very-nice sounding, "Whatever."

CHAPTER TWELVE

FIRST VISITOR

FROM THE KITCHEN window she watched him climb out of the white camper he'd parked in the driveway. He walked slowly over to the fence. Next, he looked up and down the pasture with one hand over his eyes as a shield from the bright morning sun. He was a little taller than her dad, dressed in the usual country attire of jeans, shirt, and boots. From the back she could see his grayish looking hair pulled into a pony tail tied at the neck. Joe-Many-Horses was what Dad called him. She wondered what this Yakama Indian man could do to help her dad. He sure was here early. She had barely finished breakfast.

Whoa, what was that? She saw Close come galloping from the far end of the pasture and stop directly in front of the man. Close shook her head up and down and snorted a greeting as if she knew him. She had never done that for anyone else. A little feeling of jealousy came over Mandy. Close, her horse, was always at the door when she came out. Now her beloved horse was paying attention to someone else. What would happen if he accidentally touched the crescent on Close's head and discovered the 'zing'? She had to see about this.

Out the kitchen door she ran with Promise right behind her. Promise, wagging her tail, ran straight for the man and barked a greeting as if she too knew him. Mandy watched, startled by the attention her horse and dog were giving this stranger. What was going on here?

The man bent down to pet Promise then raised both arms to touch Close. To her great relief, he merely scratched behind the horse's ears. It was obvious by the way Close stood she enjoyed the contact with this man.

He heard her coming and with one hand still on Close, turned and said in a soft-spoken voice, "Hello, Amanda. I know about your beautiful horse Close, and your dad told me about this miracle dog of yours too. I think you're a lucky young lady and so are they."

The face that turned to her gave her a jolt. This was the man her dad had told her about. His dark eyes and high cheekbones were Indian, but she was struck by his look of extraordinary peace. His look almost blew her away. It was like he viewed everything around him with an inner sense of deep kindness. Without a doubt she instantly trusted this man standing before her.

"Yes," Mandy said, "Dad told me about you too. He told me your name is Joe-Many-Horses and that you're a Yakama Indian. Oops, pardon me, I'm supposed to say Native American," she corrected.

At that he smiled and said, "Amanda, think about this. We're all Native Americans if we were born in this country. It may be politically correct for some, but for me, I'm a Yakama Indian. You will have to ask each tribe member what they want to be called. For me, I am proud of my Indian heritage and very proud to be Yakama Indian. My name is Joe Earl. Joe-Many-Horses is my Indian name."

"Then how did you get the name Joe-Many-Horses?" asked Mandy.

"Because my name is Joe and I once had many horses," he said.

Mandy burst into laughter.

"Look," he said, laughing with her and pointing at the horse, "your horse thinks it's funny too. See, she's smiling."

Mandy grinned back, pleased that someone else recognized Close's smile, and started laughing again. "Wait! Stop! Please don't make me laugh anymore. Wait 'til I get up on Close," she said.

Joe led Close to the fence so Mandy could climb on. Perched on top of Close she looked down on the handsome Indian who was holding the bridle. "Tell me about your horses. And I like your Indian name. If you don't care I'll call you Joe-Many-Horses from now on. Is that okay? You can call me Mandy."

He nodded. "There is too much to tell about horses. I grew up on the reservation and helped my father raise and trade rope ponies. What I will say for now is that horses are smarter than most people think. That's why they call it *horse sense*. A horse knows the sound of its owner's voice and can recognize other sounds and words as well. Always remember to be the leader of your horse and know that your horse will take you home. A horse will guide you to your destiny if you can understand. They will tell you if you listen, but there will be another time for us to talk about horses. For now," he said, turning to go, "I'll let you have your time with your Close."

She didn't want him to leave. "Dad told me you'd be out today to check about a well, Joe-Many-Horses."

"He's right. I came out to look around the property for a possible well site," he said. "Your dad thinks he might need another well soon and I came to find a possible location."

"How do you that?" Mandy asked.

"By dowsing," said Joe-Many-Horses.

"Dowsing? What's that? I've never heard of dowsing."

"Dowsing is a way of searching for underground sources of water or metals, by use of a dowsing rod or a pendulum like this." From his pocket he pulled out a small, three-inch chain with an arrowhead on the end. "This pendulum also has other uses. It can be used for determining soil content, lost persons, and is used for health reasons too."

Mandy was intrigued. "Wow, that sounds like magic."

"That's what a lot of people think," he replied. "Dowsing is a method of tapping into the vibration of things. The act of dowsing is very ancient. It's been and is still used by peoples all over the world. You see, everything has energy and vibration. You're energy, Close is energy. Even this weed here is energy," he said as he pulled up a weed next to his boot. "The pendulum or a dowsing rod helps me respond to the vibration of the water energy underground."

"Cool, I didn't know all that was possible," Mandy said. "Is that the way well-diggers find water?"

"Some do," he said. "Many people don't believe in dowsing in spite of the fact it's been used for thousands of years. If you're interested, look up American Society of Dowsers on your computer. There are 69 chapters all over the country where people learn about electromagnetic energy fields."

Joe picked up the weed he had pulled, bent it into a y-shape, and held it before him. "This weed is an example of a dowsing rod," he said. "A forked branch of a tree works too. You hold it before you at waist level and slowly move forward. If there is water below, the rod will respond to the vibration and bend up and down like this."

Mandy watched, fascinated, as he made the weed shake in his hand.

"When you can feel the pull on the rod you know you've got something," he said.

"That's awesome," Mandy said. "I've never seen anything like that before. Can anyone do it?" she asked.

"One must practice and want to learn. It helps if a dowser learns about the flow of underground water and can study a geological map of the area. Some are better at it than others, but that's the business I do around here. I will not be dowsing here today, but when I return you may come along and watch if you like."

Mandy allowed that she would like to learn more about dowsing the next time he came back and she was hoping it would be soon.

"Before I go now, I will tell you something else. It's about your horse," Joe-Many-Horses said seriously, looking at Mandy still atop Close. "I sense your Close has a special, almost magical energy about her. Not many animals have this gift. Look at her now. She's listening to what I'm saying. I can tell by the way she's moving and twitching her ears. She knows it too. She's a very smart horse."

Mandy leaned forward on Close and patted each side of her neck. "I'm glad to hear you say that, Joe-Many-Horses. That's what I believe too," she said proudly.

"I could tell right away there was something different about your horse when I first loaded her into the trailer to bring her here," he said. "I have worked with many horses in my lifetime and I know the difference. Some humans have it and animals too. It's a rare gift that may come and go. I feel strongly your horse has this ability and I'm glad you know it too. It will be up to you to recognize and guide your horse with this special gift."

Mandy felt little chills all over her body. She was absolutely stunned by the words coming from this man. Here was someone who understood exactly what she believed about Close. So it was true. There really was something special about her horse. What she sensed about Close had just been confirmed by Joe-Many-Horses. Mandy felt a renewed sense of faith in herself and more confident about the love connection she had with her horse.

"I will tell you one more thing, Mandy, before I go," Joe-Many-Horses said. "Whatever you call this gift of your horse, magic or healing energy, always remember this. It is to be used very carefully, because...*Magic is for when you need it.*"

Chapter Thirteen

Next Visitor

"WHAT AM I supposed to wear tonight?" called out a grumpy Mandy. She did not feel like going out this evening. After the meeting with Joe-Many-Horses and being outside all day with Close, she'd rather stay home and watch TV. Besides, she was still thinking about Rick and all the things Joe-Many-Horses had told her.

"Wear something pretty," Dad yelled back. "No jeans. We're going to a nice place for dinner."

"Yeah, whatever," she said to herself, pawing through the closet. She definitely was not looking forward to dinner tonight with Dad and another woman. By going she felt disloyal to her mother and knew it would be a dull evening.

"What does he mean by *nice* anyway?" Mandy asked Promise, who was sitting on her bed with ears perked up. Searching in her closet she picked out a short pink skirt and white, short-sleeved blouse with some pink sequined flowers on the front. It was the only good outfit she'd brought, knowing she wouldn't be dressing up too often at her dad's place. "Hey, Promise, do you think Dad will think this is *nice* enough?"

Two sharp barks and a tail thumping on the bed was the answer from her dog. "Thanks, Promise, you sweet dog," she said reaching over to plant a quick kiss on her nose. "I'll tell Dad you like what I'm wearing." Slowly she brushed her brown hair straight down with bangs to the side. She noticed her hair had lightened a lot and thought it was from being in the sun so much with Close. Mandy took her time getting ready. She knew she was irritating her dad by being a slowpoke and didn't care.

"Hurry up, Mandy. Ellie just drove in and we have reservations for dinner."

"Yeah, I'm coming." To Promise who was still on the bed, Mandy said, "Don't worry, Promise. I'll be nice to the lady, but I don't have to like her. Come on, let's go."

"Why, Mandy, you're beautiful," were the first words she heard from Ellie as she came down the stairs into the living room with Promise.

Mandy felt herself blushing at the unexpected compliment which surprised her. She wondered if Ellie was just saying that for Dad's sake.

"Your dad told me all about you and your horse and your dog. He's very proud of you and loves having you here," she said.

"Thank you," Mandy said politely. At least she was saying all the right things. For a first impression she had to admit this lady was cool looking with her stylish, brown hair and pretty clothes. Her smile and eyes were friendly too. In a strange way Ellie reminded her of her mother a little bit. She wondered if this was why her dad was attracted to this lady. Still, Mandy had nagging feelings of resentment about the arrangement. She'd wait to see how the evening turned out.

The nice place her dad promised turned out to be the beautiful Cedars Restaurant on Clover Island on the Columbia River. The three of them were escorted to a window table with a wide view of the river. *This really is a nice place,* Mandy decided. She was glad she had chosen to wear her pink outfit.

A handsome young waiter greeted them, complimented Mandy and Ellie on how lovely they both looked, and took their orders. No macaroni and cheese tonight, she decided, and ordered a steak dinner thinking she could take leftovers home for Promise.

With their orders placed, Dad and Ellie began talking about local events and the people they both knew. Mandy listened, but was bored and kept looking out the window. She watched a couple dock their boat and come into the restaurant. *What a way to arrive for dinner,* she thought. While her dad and Ellie kept talking, she watched the boats on the river and thought more about Ria and Rick. She wondered what might happen to Rick and his family.

Ellie looked over at Mandy and changed the subject. "Pardon me, but I have to tell you both about the crazy thing that happened the other day. It's about my neighbor's two goats, Flash and Dash. You see, my neighbor Mr. Kees keeps them because they're good companions for his horses, plus they eat the weeds around his place. I don't know if you know this," she said, "but goats are like weed whackers and lawn mowers. They will eat just about anything. Well, the other afternoon I was napping on the sofa in the living room. I don't know how in the world they did it, but Flash and Dash figured out how to open the screen door on the back porch and they came right inside my house. First, they ate the bedding plants I had set out on the porch. Next, they went into the living room and ate the bottom leaves off of some of my house plants. Now, get this! After that they both started chewing on my shorts…while I was sleeping! Can you believe it?"

Mandy couldn't help it. She started to laugh. The evening was starting to be fun and her dad began to chuckle too.

"I honestly thought I was dreaming or having a daytime nightmare," Ellie said. "What I heard was this soft munch-munch-munch sound and a gentle pulling on the hem of my shorts. When I finally opened my eyes there were these two white faces with whiskers under their chins staring back at me. They were just chewing away happy as could be. I came up off that sofa with a yelp so loud it sent Flash and Dash flashing and dashing right out the back door. Now I have to ask you both, I need your advice. Do you think I have a chance with the insurance company if I put in a claim for my plants and pants because they were eaten by two goat burglars?"

That brought even more hilarious laughter from Mandy and her dad, who were both holding napkins to their faces from laughing so hard. The whole evening was progressing far better than Mandy ever imagined. She was having a good time and she could tell Dad was very happy too. She noticed his eyes sparkled when he looked at Ellie and he acted softer around her. There was no doubt her dad liked Ellie a whole lot. She couldn't remember him ever acting like that around her mother, and the thought made her feel a little sad.

Dinner was almost over when Ellie brought up the subject of Rick Martinez. "Cancer is pretty tough for a kid of his age, or for anyone that matter," she said. "The family is upbeat and positive about Rick, but I know they're very worried. That Rick is such a great kid. His dad told me he's been out working in the fields since he was five years old. I hear he's popular at school too and pretty good at baseball. He hopes to win a baseball scholarship someday. You never know, maybe he can beat the cancer thing. I sure hope so."

It was the way Ellie talked about Rick and the Martinez family that totally changed Mandy's mind about her right then and there. She heard the honest concern in Ellie's voice and how she really cared about the family. That's all it took for Mandy. After listening to her talk about Rick, she decided Ellie was one very cool lady.

While Ellie and Dad continued talking, Mandy stayed quiet. She couldn't help it, her thoughts were about Rick and along with it another thought that kept quietly popping in her head. It was the recent words of Joe-Many-Horses. "It will be up to you to recognize and guide your horse with this gift. And remember…*magic is for when you need it.*"

CHAPTER FOURTEEN

INTERESTING DAY

HAPPY FROM THE night before spent with Dad and Ellie, Mandy was excited now for the ride with Ria. Her invitation to Ria to go riding was partly to keep her from worrying about Rick and also about the fun of being on Close.

They'd agreed to meet halfway between their homes. Ria would be on her horse Fern, a brown and white, ten-year-old appaloosa. She knew Ria loved her horse Fern as much as Mandy loved Close and knew they'd have a good time.

When they met in the afternoon, Ria's horse Fern and Close gave each other friendly snorts, which caused Mandy and Ria to laugh and copy their sounds amid wild giggles. There were more laughs when Mandy told her it looked like someone had sprinkled powered sugar all over Fern's back. After poking fun at each other's helmets, the girls began their ride on a dirt road that was safe and easy on the horses. Side by side with the reins loosely in their hands, they rode leisurely along in the afternoon sun. Summer smells from the orchards and a new cutting of hay floated up to welcome them as they rode and talked.

"How's Rick today?" Mandy asked.

"He was still asleep when I left home," she said. "He sleeps a lot these days. I think he was a little jealous when I told him we were going riding together. He loves our Fern, but he doesn't feel comfortable on a horse anymore. Our folks are still waiting for more tests results and it's taking longer than we thought. I hope you don't mind, Mandy, but I told Rick you'd be riding by today on Close. He wanted to know exactly what time. I think he wanted to be ready to look good for you. I think he likes you," she giggled.

"Yeah, that's cool," Mandy said. Her heart beat a little faster at the news and wished she'd worn a different tee shirt. "I haven't seen him yet this summer."

They continued on the dirt road that wound around neighboring pastures and farms, laughing and talking about their lives. Mandy told Ria about the dinner she had with her dad and Ellie and some news about her mom and Alex. They talked about their schools in Kennewick and Spokane

"How do you like your school, Ria?" Mandy asked.

"Oh, the kids at Finley Middle School are friendly and they have some real cool programs. I like the teachers I'll have this fall and so far everything's okay. What about you?"

"I'll be starting at Sacagawea in Spokane and it's going to be different because now I'll have to take a bus to school. Hey, stop a second," Mandy said and pointed toward the fence. "What kind of horses are those over there, Ria? Do you know? They're awesome looking. They look a little like Close."

"Yeah," said Ria, "those are Thoroughbred horses and they belong to Mr. Henry Dolan, your neighbor."

"Oh, those must be the horses Doc Barnes was telling us about," Mandy said.

"Papa knows him and says his place is kind of a breeding ranch. He says Mr. Dolan comes from California and travels around the country to buy expensive stallions. Then he breeds them with mares from famous racing stock right here on his ranch."

"Why does he do that?"

"Papa says he plans to come up with what's called a 'designer colt' that's supposed to end up being a super winner in big horse races. Papa says he's very rich and he's good to his horses and workers. Some of our Mexican friends work for him and he's helping them become US citizens."

The sound of a vehicle behind them caused Ria to move her horse behind Close. An older, white pickup truck slowed down as it passed them. Two men inside turned their heads and stared hard at their horses as they drove by.

"Hey, Ria," Mandy called back, "do you know those guys?"

"No, I don't," she said. "Not too many people drive down here. They probably took the wrong road and they're lost."

"Hold it a minute, Ria," Mandy said, stopping Close and pulling out her cell phone. "I almost forgot. I'd better call Dad. He knows we're riding together. I need to tell him I'll be stopping at your place later. You know how freaked out dads get when you don't let them know where you are every minute."

"Yeah, my papa's weird about that stuff too. I guess they think we can't take care of ourselves," said Ria.

While Mandy was on her cell phone the same pickup passed them again, going much slower than before. This time the men stared longer at the horses, then sped out of sight, leaving the girls and horses in a cloud of chalky dust.

"Ria, did you see that?" Mandy asked, looking behind her and coughing from the dust. "There they go again. They were watching our horses, weren't they? Why do you think they were doing that?"

"I don't know. They looked like a couple of dorks to me. They sure weren't looking at us. They were only looking at our horses," Ria said. "Did you tell your dad?"

"No, the line was busy. I'll try him later."

"I don't know about you," said Ria, "but I don't feel good about that truck, and those guys looked too creepy. Let's get out of here. Follow me. We'll take the road on the left up ahead. The road is better there and it goes right past our place."

"Good. That pickup driving by didn't feel right to me either. I don't like the way they were looking at our horses," Mandy said.

"It was weird," said Ria.

The girls urged their horses to speed up as they took the road on the left. They kept watching in case the pickup returned, but no other vehicle appeared.

The closer they rode to the Martinez place the more Mandy thought of Rick. She wondered why she was thinking so strongly about him. In a way she was excited to see him because she liked him and thought he was cool. Maybe his cancer wasn't as bad as everyone thought. She'd know more when she saw him.

Ria led as they rode up the long driveway toward the Martinez farm house. Thinking Rick might be outside, Mandy looked around the yard to spot him. He was outside all right, but not how she expected. He was sitting limply in an old chair by the side of the house and did not look well at all. A heavy sweater was draped over his shoulders in spite of the warm day. Mandy always thought Rick, who was slim and taller than most boys his age, was movie-star handsome with his black hair and dark eyes. Today he looked pale and weak. This was not the Rick she remembered and felt saddened by his appearance.

"Hi, Ricardo, how's it going?" she called out to him, trying to sound cheery.

"Buenos dias, Mandy. Nice to see you. I hear you're staying longer than two weeks this year. Is that so?"

"Yes," said Mandy. "Dad has to put up with me all summer, so he gave me my own horse. How is it with you? How are you feeling?"

"Oh some days are good, some not so good, and the bad days suck. The last we heard there was some problem with my tests. That means I have to go back again. That part's not fun, but I can tell you right now I plan to get well," said Rick. "That's a promise," he added, sitting a little straighter in his chair.

"Good for you, Rick."

"The doctors had better get me fixed up pretty quick because I start Kennewick High next month and I don't want to miss a day. I'm hoping to get on the baseball team, and Papa needs my help here on the farm too. I have to get well, that's for sure. Come on, now. Show me your horse."

Mandy slid off Close and led her a little nearer to Rick, thinking that seeing her horse might make him feel a little better. While she smoothed Close's neck she told them both about finding Promise. She gave no hint of the special healing that had happened to the dog. They asked questions about Close and she told them the story about how her dad had found the horse. Both cheered when Mandy told how Close refused to get into the truck headed for the slaughter house but went right into Joe-Many-Horse's trailer. They called out, "Way to go, Close, way to go!" Mandy saw Rick look at Close in a new admiring way.

"Don't leave yet, Mandy," Ria said. "I'm going to take Fern back to the pasture and take off her bridle. I'll be right back."

After Ria was gone Rick said, "Hey, Mandy, bring Close over here. I want a good look at that gutsy horse of yours."

Rick sounds so brave, Mandy thought. It was quite clear he really wanted to get well. With the reins in her hand she said, "Close, come meet Rick. He likes horses and you'll like him too."

The closer she moved toward Rick the stronger the words, *Magic is for when you need it,* began throbbing in her head. A strange feeling came over her. There was no question; she knew exactly what she had to do. Mandy guided Close to stand directly in front of Rick's chair. Close moved as directed and looked down at Rick. Without a word, Rick looked up at Close and slowly pulled himself up. Almost as if his arm were guided, Rick reached straight up to touch Close's head. A breathless "oh" was the only sound from Rick as his hand made contact with the white crescent on the horse's head. Mandy, with one hand holding the reins, the other on Close's neck, felt the strong connection she had come to know from her horse.

She did not know how long the three of them stood in that position. It ended when Rick, without a word, dropped his arm and sank back into his chair.

From Close came a soft, moan-like sound Mandy had never heard before. It was a strangely beautiful sound. It felt like a flow of love-music from the heart of her horse. She said nothing and looked at Rick, hoping with all her heart that he had felt it too.

looking. I don't mean that your truck is beat-up looking or anything." She smiled.

"Go on."

"It had a trailer hitch on the back," Mandy said, "and when it passed the second time I noticed a hub cap missing on the back tire."

"That's good, Mandy. Now tell me, what did the guys look like?"

She went on to described the guys as youngish looking, wearing white tee shirts and western hats. One guy was white, the other one was more suntanned. The real reason she noticed everything was because it involved the horses. She wasn't sure how important all this information was, but her dad seemed to think it was.

"Tell me more," Dad said. "Were their windows rolled down? Could you hear them talking to each other? What did they say?"

"Their windows were rolled down," said Mandy. "No, they weren't talking. They were too busy looking at Close and Fern."

"Now listen here, Mandy. If you ever see that truck or those guys again you're to call me immediately. Do you understand?"

"I did call you. I carry my cell phone with me all the time. Like I said, the line was busy."

"Then you should have kept trying. I don't talk that long. You should have called me about those guys right then and there."

"Why, what are you thinking?" Mandy asked, now feeling a little anxious.

"I'll look into that later, but..." The conversation was interrupted by the sound of his phone.

But what? Mandy wondered as her dad picked up the phone. Dad wouldn't have asked all those questions if he hadn't been concerned about the truck passing them. He acted as if he suspected something. At least he didn't ask about the rest of the afternoon. For sure she was not going to tell him about Rick and Close. She stood and listened to the rest of the phone call.

"When did it happen? How bad is it? Yeah, okay. Thanks for calling, Rodrigo. I'll be over in a little while and take a look at it. Don't worry, I'll take care of it." He put the phone down. "Hmm, I wonder how that happened?" Dad said.

"What happened?" asked Mandy. "And who's Rodrigo?"

"He's one of the trainers from the Dolan place. He said a fence post that borders our properties needs fixing and that I should come look at it. That's strange. I check my fences all the time. There was nothing wrong with it a few days ago. Oh well," he said, "that's what happens when you have animals and fences. Animals always want to know what's on the other side. I guess I'd better go check it out."

"Can I go along? I'd love to see those Thoroughbreds up close," Mandy said. "Ria told me about them today on our ride. Can I take Promise with us?"

"Come on and put your boots on. We'll be walking out in the pasture and no, Promise stays here. They have their own dogs."

Mandy grabbed her boots from the closet. "Dad, wait. This will only take a minute. I want to try something. I'm going to sneak out the front door and get into the truck where Close can't see me. I want to see if she really knows when I leave the house. Look, she's way over there eating grass and can't see me. I want to know for sure if she can tell when I go outside."

"All right, but hurry up. I want to get this fence thing taken care of now."

Mandy went out the front door and tiptoed around the side of the house, keeping her head down along the way. She had no sooner opened the door on her side of the truck when she heard a whinny. Peeking through the truck window she watched her beautiful Close trotting to the fence, tossing mane and tail. Mandy ran around the side of the truck toward the fence. "Oh, Close, how did you know I was outside? Dad," called Mandy, "here's Close! Did you see that? She does know, she did it again."

Close thrust her head over the fence so Mandy could reach her. "Close, you were awesome today with Rick. We tried our best, didn't we? I'm so sorry it didn't work for him. Anyway, you really do know when I come outside, don't you?" she said, receiving a horsy kiss in reply. "How do you do that, you smart horse?"

Without question, Mandy knew because of the almost magical connection between them, Close would always know when she was near.

A short distance away, someone else in a truck on a cell phone also knew Mandy and Close were near.... "Okay, Dirk, we found the one with the crescent on its head. It was just about where you said. It was being ridden by a young gal who was riding with another gal. The horse looks pretty good too, but we'll fix that. Now that we know where it is, we can add it to our next load to Canada. After we git it, we'll take it to that barn you told us about first. It'll bring in some good bucks for us this time."

CHAPTER SIXTEEN

UNEXPECTED NEWS

"WHAT'S THE BIG deal about an old fence post?" Mandy asked. "Can't they take care of that themselves?

"You don't understand. There's an old saying about 'good fences make good neighbors.' And that's why we're here, Mandy Dear."

The Dolan ranch also had a view of the Columbia River. The house was ranch style with two large, newly painted barns in back. A white fence in front framed a long, sloping lawn that looked like it had just been mowed.

"Wow, look at that. Ria says Mr. Dolan is very rich. She said he's helping some of their Mexican friends become US citizens. They work in his house and look after the horses, and she said they like working for him too."

"Is that so? Well, here we are."

Mandy pointed to the Thoroughbred horses in the back pasture. "See, Dad, over there. Those are the horses we saw today…cool, huh?"

Walking up to greet them was a middle-aged Mexican man who had the widest smile Mandy had ever seen.

"Buenos dias Mr. Bill. Nice to see you again and thanks for coming. Mr. Henry would like you to see the fence. Please, it's over here," he said as he pointed the direction.

Mandy and her dad followed Rodrigo past the well-kept barns and stables to the pasture. "Dad, look at this place. It's way huge!"

"Compared to our place it sure is," he said.

From this view, Mandy could see the top half of her dad's house in the distance. In between were fences, lots of grass, and horses. *What a great place for horses to live,* she thought and was glad her Close had all the space and grass she needed.

"This must be the one in question," said Dad, wiggling a crooked post. "It doesn't look too bad. I wonder how it happened?"

"I can answer that," a voice called out from behind them.

Mandy and her dad turned to see their neighbor, Henry Dolan, walking toward them. *This older man looks pretty good,* she thought, with his thick, white, wavy hair and friendly smile.

"First of all, let me introduce myself. I'm Henry Dolan. We met awhile back, Bill, but I haven't met this young lady yet," he said, turning to Mandy. "I can tell right away you like horses…right?"

"Right," said Mandy. "I can see you have some really cool ones too, Mr. Dolan."

"Thank you," he said. "You're welcome to come by and take a look at them anytime you like. There's always someone here who'll show you around."

"Thanks," she said and began to walk along with her dad, listening to them both talking about the fence.

"Let me explain about the fence," Henry Dolan said. "To be perfectly honest, it was my horse Done Good who knocked the post loose. He did it to get to that great-looking mare of yours who was obviously in heat. It's our fault. He shouldn't have been near your property. He's usually on the other side of the barn behind our eight-foot plank fence where he can't get to any horse in heat. Unfortunately, one of the stable boys brought him around on this side and he made a flying leap to get to your horse and did. Luckily, there's no great damage to your fence and none to the horses I'm happy to report. However, I have to tell you...I'd bet the farm your mare is now pregnant."

"You mean Close is going to have a baby?" Mandy burst out.

Both men turned to Mandy and laughed as Dad corrected her. "Come on, Mandy, you know better than that. If Close is in foal she will give birth to a colt or a filly, not a baby."

"Okay, Dad, I know what they're called, just kidding. I just like the sound of Close having a baby. It's easy to say. That's all."

Mr. Dolan and Dad smiled and nodded.

"Sorry," Henry Dolan said, "it looks like Done Good done bad when he jumped over the fence. Don't worry about the fence, Bill. I'll have it taken care of today. There is another matter I'd like to discuss with you. It's about your horse. I heard you rescued it from a slaughter-house trip to Canada. Is that true?"

"He sure did," Mandy said. "Dad saved Close."

"That's right. I bought the horse from the slaughter house guys. You probably know the ones I'm talking about."

"You bet I do," Henry Dolan said. "I know exactly the guys you're talking about. You know, you might have gotten a better deal than you think. No question your horse is a good-looking mare. When Rodrigo saw what happened he called me right away and I went out to check if your horse was hurt or injured. While examining your horse I was surprised to discover brand numbers tattooed on her upper lip. Did you know your horse once raced and has a registered pedigree?"

"What's a registered pedigree?" Mandy asked.

Henry Dolan turned to Mandy and said, "Well, young lady, I did some checking and found out your horse, Close to the Moon, was out of a mare called Moon Star and sired by a horse named Enough Is Enough. Your Close comes from famous horses."

At that moment, two horses squealing and racing in the pasture interrupted the conversation and everyone stopped to watch them. Fascinated by the horses, Mandy turned her whole attention to their wild sounds and crazy playing. As a result she barely heard the rest of the conversation between her dad and Henry Dolan.

"When I figured everything out about your horse, I decided there might be a winner there," said Henry Dolan, keeping his voice low so Mandy couldn't hear. "You know that's the business I'm in. Let me get right to the point," he said, lowering his voice even more, "I'd like to buy your horse."

"Why in the world would you want to buy a horse that was headed for the slaughter house when you can buy any horse you want?" Mandy's dad asked.

"Because I've got a gut feeling about this one and it's near by," Henry Dolan said.

"But it's not…"

"Hold on," said Dolan still speaking quietly, "I can see how your daughter feels about the horse. Here's the deal. I'll buy your horse and keep the unborn foal. I'm taking a chance on that, but as I told you I've got a gut feeling about this one. That's why I'm willing to make you a good offer. My instincts have served me well over the years and I have reason to think this one will too."

From his shirt pocket he pulled out a notebook and pencil, scribbled out some numbers, and handed it to Mandy's dad. "Plus," he said, nodding toward Mandy who was still engrossed with the horses, "she can choose a horse from any of three mares I've got and can visit Close any time she likes. How's that?"

"What I'm trying to tell you is that Close is not…"

At the sound of the name Close, Mandy turned toward the men in time to hear Mr. Dolan say, "No, no, just think about it and get back to me later."

What was that all about? she wondered. *What did Mr. Dolan want Dad to think about anyway?* Mandy was sorry she hadn't paid more attention to what they were saying. Oh well, she'd find out later.

"If it's okay with you both," Mr. Dolan said, "I'll have Doc Barnes check your horse. There'll be no expense to you. I'm responsible for what happened. He'll be able to tell us in a couple of weeks if Close is in foal. Don't worry, there's plenty of time if it's true. It'll be months before the foal would be born anyway."

Mandy saw the wink and nod Mr. Dolan gave her dad and wondered again what was going on between them. Why hadn't she listened more to what they were saying?

The next hour was spent on a tour of the place with Henry Dolan answering questions about the history of his race horses. Mandy learned more about the Thoroughbreds and was delighted to learn of Close's real name, Close to the Moon. She privately decided that made her horse as important as Mr. Dolan's Thoroughbreds.

After goodbyes and thanks to Mr. Dolan and Rodrigo they walked back to the truck. On the way home Mandy said, "That sure was interesting stuff about all his Thoroughbreds, and by the way Dad, what were you and Mr. Dolan talking about? I didn't hear everything because I was watching those horses. All I heard was something about Close. What did he mean when he asked you to think it over and get back to him with an answer?"

"I'll tell you about it later," he said without looking at her and started the truck.

His answer and the way he said it made her feel slightly uneasy. That feeling was quickly forgotten as she thought of the possibility of her horse being in foal. Wow! She could hardly wait to call Ria and tell her the news.

CHAPTER SEVENTEEN

AN ANNOUNCEMENT

"CLOSE IS PREGNANT! Yahoo! Wait 'til Ria hears this," said an excited Mandy with a phone and seat belt in each hand. "Dad, excuse me, I've got to call Ria right now and tell her Close is pregnant. She'll freak out when she hears this. Then tell me what Mr. Dolan was talking about."

"We're almost home. Please wait a few minutes, Mandy," said her dad in a serious tone. "Remember when you talk to her, your horse is in foal. Close is in foal and I want to talk to you now."

"It will just take a second. I won't be long, honest," Mandy said.

"No, Mandy," was his firm reply. "You can call her later. I want you to listen to me now and I won't take long either."

"Oops," said Mandy, "that's my phone. I think I know who it is. Hi Ria, I thought it was you. I was just going to call you. Guess what? I have some really cooooool news to tell you. Because you're my good friend, you get to hear it first. Are you ready? This will come as quite a shock to you I know, but I just found out this afternoon...are you ready? I'm going to have a baby!"

Explosive giggles from Mandy rocked the truck, causing even her dad to burst out in a loud laugh. The conversation and laughter between the two continued as Mandy excitedly told Ria all about the visit to the Dolan's ranch, the broken fence, the stallion, and Close. There was more laughter, then a pause while Mandy just listened. "Oh, Ria, cool. No problem. I'll ask Dad, and I think Friday will be fine. I've got some stuff to do around here for the rest of the week anyway. If it's okay with Dad I'll ride over Friday afternoon. Oh, by the way, thanks for riding with me today, and I did tell Dad about the truck passing us. Be sure to tell Rick I'm expecting," giggled Mandy, "then tell me what he says later. Okay? See ya, bye."

"What was that all about? What are you supposed to ask me?" asked her dad as he pulled into their driveway.

Mandy told him that Ria had invited her to ride over and watch a new DVD with her and Rick on Friday afternoon if that was okay. He nodded an approval.

Now in their driveway, Mandy unbuckled her seat belt as she watched her beautiful Close trot gracefully over to the fence. "Dad," said Mandy, her thoughts distracted, "what was it you wanted to talk to me about?"

"Oh," said her dad, looking straight ahead and avoiding her eyes, "I guess it really wasn't all that important after all. It can wait. I've some phone calls I need to make now. You sure had me laughing there, Mandy Dear. Go now. Close is waiting for you. We'll talk later."

Mandy had a phone call to make too, one she could make while standing next to her horse. She wasn't finished having fun with the fact that Close could be pregnant. With her hand smoothing Close's neck, she whispered into her cell phone, "Mom!"

"Hi, honey, how are you?" said her mother.

"Fine, Mom, except..."

"Except what? What is it this time, Mandy?" asked her mother sounding concerned. "You're not under a horse again, are you?"

"No, Mom. I don't want you to get upset when I tell you this, but..."

"But what?" demanded Mom. "What am I *not* supposed to be upset about?"

"This will come as a great surprise to you, Mom, but I'm proud to announce that... you're going to be a grandmother!"

"What?" yelled her mother, loudly over the phone. "Mandy, what in the world are you talking about? You had better be kidding! Where's your dad? I want to speak to him right now!"

Her mother's response caused a bubble of laughter from Mandy so great she had to hang onto Close. A whinny from her horse made her laugh even harder. "Mom, my Close is pregnant," she said. "She's in foal. I mean I'm going to have a little baby horse. I just had to let you know that you're going to be a grandmother."

"Oh," said Mom, now laughing along with Mandy. "I'm relieved I must say. You sure do have me going with some of your crazy phone calls. Congratulations on your baby horse. Tell me more now that I know I'm going to be a grandmother and will have a 'grand horse.' I'll have something to brag about now at the office."

"First, is Alex there? I want to tell him he's going to be an uncle."

Her mother told her that Alex wasn't home at the moment and was pretty excited because he was signed up for two weeks of soccer camp followed by two weeks of Boy Scout Camp. Because of that, Alex would miss his summer visit with their dad. "Don't tell your dad or he'll be upset. I'll call and explain it myself so he'll understand," she said.

"Okay, Mom, I won't tell Dad, and don't you tell Alex about being an uncle. I'll text him and make it a fun message." Her call ended with more laughter between them and like all others, "Love you, and hugs to Alex and Skippy."

CHAPTER EIGHTEEN

THE FRIDAY

"YEAH, I'M LEAVING just as soon as I get my...uh... jeans zipped up," Mandy grunted into her phone.

Ria, sounding happy, said, "Well, zip up and zip over."

When she was zipped up her phone rang again. This time it was Dad. "Ellie's invited us over for a late dinner tonight. Can you be ready by six?"

"Cool, I'm about ready to ride over to the Martinez. I'll be home by then," she said. "Remember, I'm going over to watch a movie with Ria and Rick." *What a great Friday this is turning out to be,* Mandy thought.

With a few more chores completed, Mandy brought the reluctant Promise into the house, kissed her nose, grabbed her helmet, and ran outside to climb onto Close. By the snorts and fancy prancing Mandy knew Close was as eager for the ride as she was. She'd been looking forward to the visit with Ria and Rick all week and was anxious to see how Rick was doing. The ride on Close would be fun too.

It didn't take long on the same back road to reach the Martinez place. As she approached closer to their house she could see from a distance Rick sitting on the front porch. "Hey, Rick! How are you? You're looking good from way out here," yelled Mandy as she and Close started up the driveway. The nearer she got the more curious she became at Rick's appearance. This certainly was not the same Rick she had seen earlier in the week. For one thing, he wasn't wearing that heavy old sweater.

"Hi ya, Mandy! Hi ya, Close," Rick called back, standing to greet her. "I'm feeling a lot better than the last time you saw me. That's for sure. Can you tell?"

Mandy could tell all right and felt a slight jolt go through her. She noticed a pinkish color to his cheeks and a 'fresh air' look about him that hadn't been there before. Definitely there was a new positive energy about Rick that had been missing a few days ago. Even his voice sounded stronger.

Mandy held the reins a little tighter and gripped her knees to the sides of Close so she wouldn't fall off. She knew exactly what had happened to Rick. Close's magic had worked! There was no doubt. The magic had healed Rick as it had for Promise.

"Rick," Mandy choked out, trying to sound okay, "you look awesome. You don't look like you were ever sick."

"Get this," Rick said, moving toward her, "the doctor said now he's not sure about the cancer and I have to go back for more tests. He said he's never had a patient like me and that maybe his diagnosis was wrong to start with. Now I'm telling everyone I'll be well enough to start school and ready for baseball tryouts. Yahoo," he yelled as he jumped up and pumped his fists in the air, "I said I'd get well. Now look at me!"

So it worked…the magic worked. It was needed for Rick and it worked! Mandy felt almost like telling Rick it was because of Close he was better. Instead, she calmly walked Close nearer to Rick, who greeted him with a soft friendly snort.

"Look, she remembers me," said Rick, patting and stroking Close's neck. "There's something very special about your horse, Mandy. I can't explain what it is, but it's the way Close makes me feel when I'm around her and touch her. I've never had that feeling around any other person or animal. Do you know what I'm talking about?" he said.

All Mandy could do was reply with a nod of her head as she watched Rick and Close side by side. She was so overcome by the change in Rick she could hardly talk. She watched to see if he would reach for Close's magic spot again. He didn't. *Magic is for when you need it.* By the looks of Rick, he didn't need it anymore. So that's why Ria had laughed and sounded so happy on the phone today. Her brother was better.

The three of them spent so much time talking about Rick's health improvement, school, and horses that there wasn't any interest in watching a movie. They laughed more when Rick teased Mandy about having a baby and Mrs. Martinez joined in too when she heard them laughing so loud on the porch.

When it was time to leave she climbed back on Close, made plans to go riding with Ria, and told Rick how great he looked. That was the most she could say to his face. Arriving home she brushed Close more lovingly than ever and led her back out to the pasture to graze. Her sweet dog Promise was beside Close the whole time. Mandy did not say one word to either of them. There was no need. They were both tuned into her silent feelings of love.

It was six o'clock when a different-feeling Mandy and her dad left the house to meet Ellie for dinner. The sun was lower in the sky as they backed out of the driveway, catching Close in the middle of the sunset's glow. "Dad! Look!" Mandy said and pointed to her horse. "Close has a golden halo around her. The sun makes her look all golden." To herself she knew that Close truly was a golden horse.

He stopped the truck for a long look. "You're right, she does."

That would have been a golden moment to tell Dad about Rick and Close's healing, but as before, she kept silent.

"I put Promise in the house because I thought we might be late tonight," Mandy said. "Do you know what she did first? She did the weirdest thing. She kept running back and forth to Close and whining. I've never seen her do that before. She definitely didn't want to be inside and acted kind of mad at me for putting her in the house. I guess she just wanted to be with Close tonight."

Her dad nodded in agreement. "Don't worry. She'll be okay until we get home."

The evening with Ellie and her dad was perfect. Ellie prepared a meal of her own, pizza and a fresh salad of greens from her garden. Dessert was homemade apple pie topped with vanilla ice cream. After dinner they all walked over to visit with Mr. Kees and watch Flash and Dash with the horses and hear more funny stories about the goats. During the evening Mandy hoped with all her heart that Rick's name would not be mentioned for fear she'd explode with news about his healing. It was hard to keep her mouth shut, but she did. On the way home Mandy talked about what a great cook Ellie was.

"Not bad," said Dad. "You know she made that meal especially for you tonight."

"That's awesome," she said. "I wouldn't mind eating like that all the time. Oh, look out there. It looks like a full moon tonight. There it is so big and yellow."

"It sure is. Did you know the August full moon is called Dog's Day Moon or some call it the Woodcutters Moon?" Dad asked, now in the driveway. "It's almost as bright as day," he added.

"Dad, if it's so bright out then why can't I see Close?" asked an anxious Mandy, leaning out her window. "Close is always at the fence when I'm outside or when we drive home. Where is she now? I don't see her out there. Close, where are you?" yelled Mandy, jumping out of the truck and running to the gate.

Feelings of a happy day disappeared, now replaced by a growing fear.

"Close, Close!" Mandy called frantically into the night. "Close, where are you?"

Frantic barking from inside the house was the only answer to her calls.

CHAPTER NINETEEN

A CLUE

"WHERE ARE YOU, Close?" Mandy screamed, running wildly in the grassy shadows. "Where are you?" Mandy knew her horse had to be here somewhere. This was where she lived. She ran to a dip in the pasture where Close used to lie down in the grass...nothing. She ran back to see if the pasture gate was open. It was closed. Finally, after searching all over, she stopped when she realized that Close was not on the property. She bowed her head and began to sob her heart out.

Her dad, who had been searching at the other end of the pasture, came to her and put his arms around her. "Listen to me, Mandy. She's not here, but we'll find her. Don't worry. There must be reason why she's gone. We'll find out why and where and get her back. Do you hear me? Crying is not going to help. Right now I need you to be strong."

"Close is not like any other horse. You don't understand, Dad. She's very special. She can't have just disappeared. Someone must have taken her. We've got to find her!"

He gently brushed her tears away with his fingers. "I know you're hurting, but we'll figure out what to do. Don't worry," he said. "If someone has taken her we'll find out who and get her back. Okay? Come on now, dry up those tears. She can't be too far away."

"What should we do right now?" Mandy asked, wiping the last tear away. "Where do we start looking for her?"

"First of all, it's obvious Close is not on our property. We know that for sure now. There are no broken fences so she couldn't have gotten out that way. I've got an idea," he said. "Let's get Promise out here. That dog and Close are pals. Maybe there's something there."

Mandy and her dad were almost knocked over as Promise bolted through the kitchen door past them, barking loudly. First she raced to the gate, crawled under, and ran up and down the pasture along the fence barking furiously. Next, she crawled back under the gate and ran up and down the driveway howling.

Mandy watched her running and howling. Promise had never acted like that before. Maybe she knew something, but what? Now she understood why Promise rebelled at staying inside the house. She must have sensed some kind of danger to Close before it happened.

"I wonder why she keeps running up and down the drive way?" Dad said.

"Maybe she knows what happened," Mandy said, "and she's trying to tell us."

Dad nodded. "Come in the house. I need to make some phone calls. Looks like things are starting to add up."

The first call was to Joe-Many-Horses, then Henry Dolan their neighbor. He made a few more calls, with the last one to the Martinez home. When he finished, Mandy asked, "Why did you call Joe-Many-Horses? How can he help us find Close?"

"I called him because he's smart about horses and he's familiar with this whole area. Besides that, he knows how to find things. He's coming right over, Mandy. Clear off the kitchen table please. We'll need the space to work on," Dad said.

Joe-Many-Horses arrived soon, carrying a rolled-up paper. He was greeted by the worried faces of Mandy and her dad.

"Thanks for coming over so late, Joe," Mandy's dad said. "I have a hunch we have to move fast on this one. Every minute counts. What can you show us?"

"I think you're right, Bill," said Joe-Many-Horses. "Let's get started."

He unrolled the paper and spread it on the table.

"What's that?" Mandy said, looking down at the paper. "It looks like a map. How can that help us find Close? Shouldn't we be outside looking for her?"

"It's a map of the Kennewick area," Joe-Many-Horses said, spreading his hand all over the map. "I believe that your horse is somewhere in this area. She can't be too far away. I will use my pendulum to try to find where." From his breast pocket he took out the pendulum with the arrow on the end that Mandy had seen before. "First, I will clear my pendulum and focus on what we are seeking. Remember when I was here earlier and told you about dowsing and all it can do? My pendulum can do the same thing."

Mandy nodded her head.

"Next, I look at the map and put my hand over the whole area like this," he said.

Mandy and her dad watched as Joe-Many-Horses moved the palm of his hand slowly over the map.

"Then I put my finger on a place and ask the pendulum if the horse is here. First, I swing the pendulum up and down. If the pendulum swings left-to-right, the answer is 'no.' So I move my finger on the map to a different location. I keep moving my finger until the pendulum swings right-to-left. That's how my pendulum answers 'yes' to my question. It is the same way when dowsing for water. I can walk the grass or use a map."

"How do you know when you're right?" asked Mandy.

"I trust my pendulum and my own intuition. After many years of use I have learned that doubt will bring wrong information. Also, it is important to ask the right question," he continued.

"Can the pendulum tell us if we'll get Close back?" asked Mandy.

"No, a pendulum does not tell the future. That is not its purpose," said a serious Joe-Many-Horses. "Let's just focus on what we're here to do. If Close is anywhere on this map I am working with, my pendulum will guide me to the right place."

With great interest, Mandy and Dad watched every move Joe-Many-Horses made with his pendulum. Again he covered a wide area with his hand and then narrowed it down to a smaller circle. Finally, they noticed he kept moving his finger and pendulum back to the same spot on the map. Looking up from the map he said, "Bill, take a look at this. Tell me. Do you know this area?"

"You bet I do," Mandy's dad said in an excited voice. "It's a couple of miles from here on the old Hamel Road. There's a deserted barn out there on the property. Those folks haven't lived there for years and the whole place is up for sale. Come to think of it, that barn would be a perfect place to hide horses."

"Then that's it!" said Joe-Many-Horses, smiling. "My pendulum indicates that's the area to check."

An excited Mandy, with Promise right beside her, headed for the door and called back, "Dad, hurry! Let's go! We've got to find Close and bring her home!"

CHAPTER TWENTY

THE SEARCH

DUST FLEW BEHIND the truck, leaving an eerie trail in the moonlight as her dad sped down the dirt road toward the old Hamel place. It was agreed that Mandy's dad would lead in the truck and Joe-Many-Horses would follow later with the horse trailer. After three more phone calls they were on their way.

"I think I know what's going on and who's behind all this," growled her dad, "and that man is not going to get away with stealing our horse! There's a law against horse thieves."

Mandy felt that old tight feeling in her stomach again. Only this time it was about her horse. Her whole body tightened as she heard her dad's anger and determination to find whoever was responsible for stealing Close.

Promise also was tense and alert on her lap. From the dog came a deep, low, almost gurgle-like growl. "What is it, Promise?" said Mandy, stroking the dog's head. "Look, she's acting weird again. Its okay, girl, don't worry. We're on our way to find Close and bring her home."

"She senses something too," said her dad, eyes fixed straight ahead on the road. "Hang on, you two. It's just a little further. Thanks to Joe and his pendulum at least we know where to look."

"Dad, do you think the pendulum really works?"

"We're about to find out," he said. "It's been working for Joe-Many-Horses all these years. There's no reason why it shouldn't now. When we get there, Mandy, you and Promise stay in the truck. Do you hear me? I don't know what to expect. At least you'll be safe here."

"Okay," said Mandy, hugging Promise.

"We're coming up to it now."

Through the shadows of overgrown bushes and trees in the moonlight, Mandy saw the dark outline of the Hamel barn. Dad drove by slowly with the truck lights off. She pointed to the driveway. "Look! There's the pickup that passed me and Ria. It's the one I told you about. See, it's the same color and it's got a trailer hitch."

"Interesting," he said. "It's all coming together now." After a short distance he turned around and parked in a place hidden by trees with a clear view of the barn. For a long minute he sat and looked in every direction.

Mandy sat silently beside him, barely breathing wondering what he planned to do. She watched him quietly open the truck door and step out into the moonlit night.

He looked around then turned to Mandy. "Now listen," he said in a low voice, "I've decided to scout around behind the barn first to make sure Close is inside. I want to see if anyone else is poking around this place. You must be very quiet, and for heaven's sake, stay right here in this truck. Do not move from here no matter what happens. I mean it, do you understand? I don't know what's out there and I want you safe right here."

Mandy nodded her head. Seconds after her dad was gone she slowly drew a deep breath and rolled her window down all the way to listen for any sound in the quiet moonlit night. The only thing she heard was the fading crunch of her dad's boots on the gravel road and the sound of a train far in the distance. She sat like a statue with Promise beside her, just listening and looking and thinking about what might happen next.

With each passing moment Mandy began to feel more anxious. It seemed like hours since Dad had left. Finally, she could stand it no longer. She had to do something. What if Dad was in danger and needed help? Although she'd promised to stay in the truck she couldn't just sit there. She had to find out for herself what was going on. The decision was made for her by Promise, who suddenly tried to wiggle out her side window. Mandy scooped her back, then with her heart beating faster snapped on her leash and slowly opened the truck door. "Good girl, Promise. Let's go find Dad and Close," she whispered.

It was easy to find the driveway to the old house and barn. Weeds had mostly overgrown everything, but the well-worn tracks of old vehicles left an easy path to follow in the moonlight. Dark shadows from overgrown bushes on both sides of the driveway added to a scary feeling as she and Promise moved along.

Mandy tightened Promise's leash to feel the safety of the dog next to her leg. Promise strained harder on the leash, and Mandy found herself being pulled along as Promise headed straight for the dark barn.

"Stop, Promise," she said quietly, tugging hard on the leash. She looked around There was no sound or movement of any kind, only the unfriendly looking shadows. *Where is Dad?* she thought. *Could he be in danger? Why hasn't he come back to the truck? Where is Joe-Many-Horses? He was supposed to follow us.* For a second, she almost wished she had stayed in the truck, but she couldn't go back now. Promise had pulled her right to the barn door. No matter what, she had to find her dad and Close. She looked at the barn door, trying to decide what to do. It just made sense to look inside. Mandy took a step forward to lean a little on the door to see if it would open easily. When it didn't, her heart racing, she reached for the handle.

Suddenly, without warning, the barn door opened. Mandy jumped back, almost falling on Promise who gave a small yelp. In the darkened doorway a large dark shadow making no sound began moving toward her. That's when she saw it…shining in the moonlight…a belt buckle with the words "Bad Company." It was Dirk looking down at her. With a surprising instant strength and courage Mandy lunged forward. "Where's my horse? I want her back!" she demanded. "What have you done with her?"

Dirk, not moving, looked straight down at Mandy and Promise. "Whoa now," he said in a cocky voice, "what do we have here? Oh, I know who you are. You're that kid of the Hawkins guy, the one who took a horse from me. Just what do you think you're doing here late at night with that mutt all by yourself? It's dangerous here, little lady. You could get hurt and no one would find out for a long time. And I don't know a thing about your horse, either."

There was no mistake. Mandy knew in her heart this was the man who had taken Close. With a courage still streaming she yelled at him, "I know you've got my horse and I want her back. You had no right to take her!"

"Why, you little brat, you don't know what you're talking about. You'd better get the heck out of here before I…"

"Before you what?" challenged a loud voice coming from around the corner of the barn.

Mandy turned in surprise and relief as Dad stepped forward from the dark to stand beside her. "Remember me, Dirk?" said her dad with his hand now safely on Mandy's shoulder.

"Oh, Dad," Mandy sighed, "thank goodness you're okay!"

Dirk glowered at both of them. "Yeah, I sure do remember you and you'd better take that nosey kid of yours and get the heck out of here."

"We sure will, just as soon we get our horse out of the barn."

"Well, ain't we a smart one tonight, Bill Hawkins? I don't know a thing about your darn horse, and it's none of your business what I've got in the barn, so git!"

"Oh come on, Dirk, let's get something straight. You know perfectly well which horse I'm talking about, and I want her now!" her dad said louder. "So come on. Why don't we go take a look in the barn?"

Mandy, heart pounding, was still holding tightly to Promise, who began a low, menacing growl at Dirk.

"What in the name of you-know-what makes you think I'll take you back there?" snarled Dirk. "This is private property, and you got no right to be here."

"You've got that one right," said Mandy's dad. "It sure is private property. I made a few phone calls before I came out here and found out this ranch still belongs to the Hamels. They're not going to be too happy when they find out you've been using their barn to hide horses. You've absolutely no business to be here. Now I want…"

"My dad's right," said a brave-sounding Mandy. "It's our horse. We know you've got her and we want her back right now."

"You can't prove I've got your stupid horse," shouted Dirk.

"Wanna bet?" said Mandy's dad. "Here's something you didn't figure on. Our horse has a tattooed registered number that proves who she was sired by. I know what the numbers are, so why don't we go back there and check. Besides, I have a bill of sale to prove I own the horse…remember? Then we'll find out who's the stupid one."

"Yeah, we've got papers to show Close is ours," Mandy said, standing beside Dad.

"We'll see who's stupid," yelled Dirk. Without warning, from his back pocket he pulled out a riding crop that had gone unnoticed in the dark. Mandy heard a crack in the air and watched in horror as Dirk aimed the whip straight at her dad.

"Dad!" screamed Mandy. "Look out!"

Her dad, caught off guard, stumbled back a little just in time to miss the first whip lash.

"Dad!" Mandy screamed louder as she watched Dirk bring his arm back to strike again. Without thinking and forgetting her own safety, Mandy rushed forward to push her dad away and dropped Promise's leash in her move. That's all it took. A flash of black and white flew past her as Promise charged Dirk. Promise leaped at him, knocked him flat on the ground, and with a death-curdling growl brought bared teeth to Dirk's throat.

"Agghh! Get away from me!" cried Dirk, desperately trying to protect himself from the attack.

"Promise!" yelled Mandy.

Her dad, now on his feet, grabbed Promise's leash and yanked her back just before she reached for the back of Dirk's neck. Promise gave a final fierce growl to Dirk, who lay on the ground holding his head.

"Get that blankety-blank dog away from me or I guarantee you'll be sorry," he yelled.

Everything had happened so quickly that Mandy didn't know what to expect next. But a noise in the driveway drew her attention. What she saw looked like a silent army of moonlit ghosts marching straight toward them.

"Is everything okay, Bill?" a voice called out. "Need any help?" Up the driveway came Joe-Many-Horses, Henry Dolan, Rodrigo, Mr. Martinez, and Doc Barnes, the friends and neighbors her dad had called.

With a huge sigh of relief and knowing Dad was totally safe, Mandy grabbed Promise's leash and followed her brave dog into the barn to find what they had come for. Stepping carefully, she entered the dark barn, where slits of moonlight shone through cracks in the boards. The strong, musty smell of old hay and horse manure greeted her and another sound…the sound of a horse…who always knew when she was near.

CHAPTER TWENTY-ONE

SAD DISCOVERY

LOUD THRASHING SOUNDS and whinnies coming from the far end of the barn sent the unleashed Promise straight for Close. Mandy, right behind, was moving more slowly as her eyes became accustomed to the darkened barn

"Close, it's Mandy. I'm coming! I'm coming!" she called as she stumbled over the litter of weathered boards and clumps of hay.

In the dim light she saw the shadow of her distressed horse trying to rear up and break free from the rope that kept her tight in a corner stall. Within seconds Mandy found her way to Close and was inside the stall to comfort her terrified horse. "There, there," said Mandy in a quivering voice as she reached for Close's halter. "Close, I'm here now. It's okay, girl. You're safe and Promise is right here beside you too. We're going home just as soon as I can get you out of here."

Close, panting heavily and snorting, stopped rearing at Mandy's familiar voice.

"Dad and I are going to take you home where you belong," she said. With one hand on the halter she tried to pull Close's head down to release the breakaway snap. With the other hand she began stroking Close's quivering neck and shoulder. That's when her fingers touched something wet and sticky. "Ugh… what's this?" she blurted out. In a horrifying instant she realized she was touching blood…Close's blood. Close was bleeding. Blood was all over her back.

"Oh," she gasped, "Close, no." In a trembling voice and trying not to cry, she said, "I'm going outside for help. I'll be gone a minute and Promise will stay here with you. I'll be right back and we'll get you fixed up. Oh, I love you, Close. You're going to be okay. Do you hear me?"

The soft nickering that came from Close was one Mandy recognized. After all the hundreds of hours she had spent with her horse she had come to know the meaning of all the different whinnies and sounds her horse made. She knew Close understood everything she had said.

With her heart pounding, Mandy made her way quickly back out of the barn. She ran for her dad, who had joined his friends surrounding the angry Dirk. "Dad," Mandy called, "come quick. Close is hurt. She's bleeding. Look, there's blood on her back," she said, holding up her bloody hand. "She's hurt real bad. Hurry! She needs help."

All eyes turned from Mandy to Dirk, who put his hands up and yelled back. "Don't look at me! I didn't do a thing to that stupid horse and you can't prove I did. Someone else must've done it. It wasn't me."

Her dad stepped away from the group to come to Mandy. With his arm around her he said, "Don't worry, Mandy. We're lucky Doc Barnes is here. He and Henry Dolan will go with you to see about Close. They'll know what to do. I'm staying right here until the sheriff comes. I don't want that dirty-so-and-so Dirk to get away until we find out what he's done. You go with them now and help them."

Flashlights were handed to Henry Dolan and Doc Barnes, who followed Mandy into the barn. When they reached the stall, Promise was inside lying beside Close, who had quieted down.

"I'm back," Mandy said, gently touching her horse's neck. "Doc Barnes is here and he's going to take a look at you. Promise and I will stay right with you. We won't leave."

Another quiet whinny was heard from the stall.

"Hold that flashlight over here, Henry," said Doc Barnes. "Let's take a look and see what we're dealing with. Well, hello," he said as the light flashed inside the stall. "We've not only got a bloody horse, but we've also got a bloody bat someone's left behind. Easy, Girl," he said as he peered closely at the horse's head and neck. "Very interesting."

Mandy stood outside the stall with arms tight around herself to keep from shaking as she watched and listened. Blood on Close meant she'd been beaten, and she was scared about what it meant for her horse. She couldn't understand what Doc Barnes was doing and his silence worried her even more. She watched him move out of the stall and heard him say quietly to Henry Dolan. "I think we'd better discuss this with Bill before we go any further. He should know what needs to be done here."

"No, first we have to let Mandy know what the situation is," said Dolan, shining the flashlight on her and speaking louder for her to hear. "It's her horse. She has the right to know first what's happened and don't worry about the bill."

"Very well," said Doc Barnes talking louder. "First off," he said turning to Mandy, "let me assure you the chances are good your horse is going to be okay. It's obvious Close has been beaten around the neck and shoulders with the bat I found. She's bleeding from the welts and needs immediate attention to clean up the wounds so there's no infection. The good news is you and your dad interrupted a horse beating that could have been much worse if you hadn't come along when you did. This is one lucky horse you've got here, Mandy."

Mandy swallowed hard, trying not to cry. Everything felt so unreal. She felt like she was outside of herself looking down on what was happening before her. She hung onto every word of Doc Barnes as he described how he was going to give Close a tranquilizer that would put her out for 30 minutes. He explained how it was necessary so he could apply a healing antiseptic before stitching up the wounds. He told her that when Close woke up she would be groggy for a bit, but soon after she would be up and around looking for something to eat.

"Close will be feeling better in no time," Doc said. "You'll see."

The positive words of Doc Barnes made Mandy feel instantly better. She felt herself beginning to relax a little.

"Come with me," he said, "we'll talk to your dad about all of this. I can start on Close just as soon as I get my things out of the van."

"Excuse me for a minute, Doc Barnes. I need to tell Close what's going to happen to her first."

The two men stepped away as Mandy entered the stall. She placed her arms lightly around Close's neck, careful to avoid the bloody area, and hugged her as gently as possible. Although Close had calmed down a little, Mandy could feel the rapid beating of her heart and a wild look still in her eyes. Softly and in trembling voice, she told her horse how sorry she was that she had been taken away and beaten. She explained to Close that Doc Barnes was going to put her to sleep for awhile so he could make her feel better. "I'll be right with you the whole time," she said. "You don't have to be scared anymore. After that, Dad will see to it no one ever hurts you again. I'm going outside with Doc Barnes and Mr. Dolan for a minute and then we'll be right back. Don't worry, Promise will stay here with you." Again, the soft snorting from Close meant she understood.

As they passed the men standing around Dirk, who was sitting on the ground, Mandy heard his words come floating out in the moonlight. "You can't prove I did one darn thing to that horse."

From behind her Doc Barnes yelled back, "That's what *you* think. We've got a pretty good witness here...and it looks like a bloody bat!"

CHAPTER TWENTY-TWO

WHEN NEEDED

THE MOON WAS lower in the sky as a weary Mandy watched her dad's friends drive away into the August night. They'd hung around discussing events of the evening and how it had happened during a full moon. She heard them talk about the heroic act of Promise, who had saved her dad and of what might happen to Dirk. To Mandy's great relief, Doc Barnes checked Close one more time before he drove away.

Last to leave was Joe-Many-Horses, who stayed around to help bring Close home in his horse trailer. Too tired to help, Mandy watched while Dad and Joe-Many-Horses gently unloaded Close from the trailer into the pasture.

Close stumbled a little until she got her footing and began walking slowly in a normal way along the fence. Promise walked along right beside her and never left her side. With head down, Close began grazing just as Doc Barnes said she would. It was a sight that filled Mandy with joy to see her beloved horse alive and home with Promise after the horrible events of the past few hours.

She watched Close a few minutes longer then walked over to say goodbye and thanks to Joe-Many-Horses. He had been right all along about finding Close at the Hamel place. His pendulum had really worked. Because of it they had arrived in time to save Close. She meant more than a "thank you" to Joe-Many-Horses, but didn't know the way to say it. Finally, she reached up and put her arms around the man's neck and said, "Thank you for saving my Close. We couldn't have found her without you." The words coming from her heart were received by him with a smile and nod of his head.

Joe-Many-Horses looked away at Close now grazing with head down. He turned back to Mandy and said softly, "You know it was because of you that Close did so well this night. She knew you were always near."

After more thanks and goodbyes to Joe-Many-Horses, Mandy and her dad walked back to check on Close. They talked again about the rescue with the help of friends and neighbors.

"That's one lucky horse out there, Mandy," said her dad, leaning on the fence. "Close was saved again. There's another thing, I want you to know how proud I am of you and that dog of yours. Tonight would have turned out differently if you two hadn't been there."

"Thanks, Dad," said Mandy, standing beside him. "That really was awesome the way Promise went after that Dirk guy. And now, if you, don't care, I want to sleep outside tonight. I want to be outside with Close and Promise."

"Are you sure? You heard Doc Barnes say Close was going to be all right. And you look like you're ready to crash."

"So do you, Dad. I'm okay. How about if I sleep in the back of the truck if you could park it next to the gate? I'll get my sleeping bag and Promise can be with me too. That way I can keep an eye on Close and she'll know where I am. Dad, I need to do this. Please, it's important."

"There's not much of tonight left and I doubt you'll be able to keep your eyes open, but if you're sure it's what you want, okay."

In a few minutes her dad had backed the pickup next to the pasture gate and Mandy was in her pajamas with sleeping bag and pillow. He helped make her bed and lifted Promise into the truck. "At least you've got a hero watch dog," Dad said, patting Promise on the nose. "I won't have to worry one bit about you." He hugged her and gave her a good-night kiss. "You won't get much sleep, Mandy Dear. In a couple of hours the sun will be in your eyes instead of the moon. Just look at Close out there. You can tell she's not groggy anymore. Considering all she's been through she looks pretty darn good. Notice how she keeps looking in your direction. She knows you're here."

"Wait, before you go in, Dad, I have to ask you something. Why did that horrible Dirk guy hurt Close and try to whip you? He made me so mad. And why did he have to hurt Close like that?"

"I'm not sure," Dad said shaking his head, "best guess is it's all about money. It started when Close wouldn't get in the horse trailer, then I came along and bought her. So he didn't get the money he was counting on. I'm thinking he decided to steal the horse and beat her up so it'd look like she was ready for the slaughter house. That way he'd get his money back. Fortunately, we came along before he could really do the job on her. That's the only thing I can figure out."

"He didn't have to try to hurt you too," Mandy said touching her dad's shoulder.

"That's the other reason. I think he was plain mad at me for getting the horse away from him and set out to get even. I came along and challenged him just when he happened to have that rider's crop in his back pocket. Anyway, the law will take care of him." With a final hug and kiss, her dad said goodnight and headed for the house, leaving Mandy with a watchful Promise beside her.

After the long day and night, Mandy was alone with her beloved horse and dog. Some of her tiredness left as she watched how much Close enjoyed the handful of hay she had brought from the barn. Standing in pajamas and slippers in the fading moonlight, Mandy began to softly stroke Close's neck, careful to avoid the stitches on her shoulder.

"Close, you're so awesome. Look up there. Tonight you really are close to the moon," she said, "just like your name says. I told you I'm sorry for all the bad things that happened to you and I'm telling you again, I'm sorry. We found you in time though, didn't we?" She told Close again how much she was loved and that as soon as she was healed they'd go riding. Mandy could sense Close relaxing around her and felt the loving connection between them as she kissed her horse on the nose. Slowly, she reached her fingers toward the crescent spot on Close's forehead, stroking her neck gently as she went along. After all that had happened tonight she could use some of the magic-like-healing energy that came from her horse.

Abruptly, Close yanked her head up and away to the side. With a soft snort and quivering of her nose, she brought her large head down on Mandy's shoulder for a fleeting second then jerked it away. Close's action totally surprised Mandy.

"Close, what's wrong? You've never done that before," she said. "Why did you do that?"

For some reason Close did not want her crescent touched. Close was trying to tell her something. Why would she not want to be touched? Mandy knew for certain the crescent was a special healing area of her horse. She had witnessed how "the touching" had healed Promise, a dying dog who was now happy, healthy, and now a hero. It had worked on Rick, who fought hard to overcome his illness so he could follow his dream to play baseball in high school. Why wasn't she allowed to feel the energy from Close now?

Standing in the fading August night next to her horse, the reason gradually came to her. She didn't need it...she had already been healed. She had been healed by Close in a different way. It came to her that her healing was the letting go of bad feelings about her parent's divorce. Old, angry thoughts about their separation had faded from her heart and mind. She realized her folks were fine just the way they were and they still loved her. There was no reason for her to ever feel that way about them again. She stood there and marveled at her change of thinking that had occurred because of Close's loving connection to her. So that was it! The magic had worked for her too and she hadn't realized it until this very night and this moment.

Close moved her head, stepped closer, flipped her tail, and with her wide intelligent eyes looked straight back at Mandy. The sound of the whinny from Close gave another reason, and Mandy knew instantly it wasn't about her this time. It was about something else. Close, by way of her special gift, was telling her...*Magic is for when you need it...and the foal growing inside needs the magic for now.*

With tears streaming down her face, Mandy gently hugged her horse. "Oh, Close girl," Mandy cried, "I'm so sorry that I didn't think about you before. Now I know, I understand beautiful Close. You've healed me too, but now you need it for you and your unborn foal. Joe-Many-Horses was right. *Magic is for when you need it,* and you need it for you this time. All of it this time, Close...the *magic* is just for you."

Q-R-T
QUICK-READ-THRU

The Columbia River

The mighty Columbia River starts in British Columbia, Canada, flows south into the state of Washington then Oregon, and finally empties into the Pacific Ocean. It is 1,243 miles long. It is the largest river in the Pacific Northwest section of North America. Did you know there are at least 12 dams on the Columbia River and some on its tributaries? It provides food, jobs, and transportation for thousands of people and has for hundreds of years. Rivers are fascination, ever-changing, and fun to learn about. Check out more facts about this great river on your computer or library and see if you can find it on the map.

The Yakama Indian Nation

In 1855 a treaty was signed that combined 14 tribes and bands of Indians into what is known as the Yakama Indian Nation. The treaty was signed near Walla Walla, Washington, and set aside 1.4 million acres to the Yakama Nation out of the original 10.8 million acres. Interestingly, the original name of the Yakamas had several meanings. One was "Tapteil" or "Wap-tail-min," meaning a "narrow river people." This refers to the Yakima River at Union Gap, where they used to set up their living sites. To learn more about the Yakama Nation, go to www.yakamamuseum.com or visit in person the Yakama Nation Cultural Center Museum at their ancestral grounds in Toppenish, Washington. There you can see how they lived, hunted, and gathered food thousands of years ago.

Dowsing and the Pendulum

Dowsing is a way of connecting into the natural vibration of an energy field such as underground water or metals by the use of a dowsing rod. A forked branch is sometimes used, and its use goes way back to 1685 in England. People from all over the world have used dowsing to find water wells. The pendulum is a smaller version of the dowsing rod used to access similar information. It takes awhile to learn how to use the pendulum correctly. For more interesting facts about dowsing, log onto the American Society of Dowsers.